ULTRA

THE LAST HERO, BOOK 1

MATT BLAKE

MATTBLAKEAUTHOR.COM

If you want to be notified when Matt Blake's next novel is released, please sign up to his mailing list.

http://mattblakeauthor.com/newsletter

Your email address will never be shared and you can unsubscribe at any time.

ULTRA

[1]

Eight Years Ago...

I'D NEVER BEEN afraid of the people with powers.

I stared out of my bedroom window. It was bright, the sun was shining strong, bouncing off the perfect white snow that I just wanted to go outside and play in. When school called and Mom told me I wouldn't be going in today, I thought at first it must be because of the snow. Which was great, because I'd waited so long for it to snow so I could go out and play in it with Brad, so I could build a snowman and play snowball fights with Cassie, if she ever got back home.

But as I looked down Sherman Avenue, I knew something was weird right away. The street was empty. People that were outside were running. They looked scared. A man and his two kids sprinted, tried not to slip on the snow. Other people closed their curtains. The Jacksons, who lived right across the road, were going out into that funny bunker thing they'd built in the garden.

I knew right then why we'd got the day off.

Something was happening with the ULTRAs.

"Oh, God. I just can't get hold of her."

"She'll be okay—"

"How the hell can you say she'll be okay, Martin?"

I heard the sounds of my mom and dad arguing, and I could tell they were scared. Scared about Cassie, probably. She was my big sister. She'd got to that age that seemed really cool to be, where you could just go off to the main Manhattan Island on the boat and spend time on your own away from Mom and Dad. I loved Mom and Dad. They looked after me and bought me cool stuff, but I liked the thought of being able to go off on my own journeys, my own adventures, just like Cassie was allowed to do. But she was fourteen, and I was only eight, so I wasn't allowed to do as much as her yet.

"Is Kyle okay?" I heard Mom say.

"Is he okay? He's in his room. Of course he's okay."

"And you know that because you've checked on him?"

"Look, Mary. We're gonna be fine. Cassie's gonna be fine. It's probably just another false flag."

I heard Mom go silent and knew that she wasn't arguing with Dad anymore. That was better. I preferred it when they weren't arguing.

I looked out of the window some more. The snow fell heavily. I just wanted to go throw some snowballs. Maybe I could sneak outside. I could be out and back before Mom and Dad even knew a thing.

I turned around and stepped over my collection of wrestling toys, walked through my room—my favorite place in the world— and got to the door. When I stepped outside it, towards the stairs, I could hear the telly booming really loud. I couldn't properly hear the words, but as I stood at the top of the stairs, I could make some of them out.

"...Breaking reports of chaos reaching New York State..."

"...Stay in your homes, ladies and gentlemen. Saint and Orion are to be avoided at all costs. Avoided at all costs..."

When I heard Saint and Orion, I felt myself get a bit excited. I knew who Saint and Orion were. They were the ULTRAs. The last two left, which saddened me a bit. They were cool. They could fly and had superpowers.

Well. Orion was cool. He liked saving people.

Saint liked killing people.

But none of them scared me.

I heard Mom and Dad chatting in the kitchen and climbed further down the stairs. I could see the snow sprinkling through the front window. The news said something about "chaos" or something coming to New York State, but I lived on Staten Island. Nothing ever happened on Staten Island.

I got to the bottom of the stairs knowing Mom and Dad would go mad if they saw me trying to leave. But I just wanted to stand in the street—just wanted to feel the snow on my face. I'd waited so long for it to snow—a whole *forever* since it snowed last year—and I wasn't gonna miss it. Not for Saint. Not for Orion. Not for any of the ULTRAs.

I walked toward the front door. Put my hand on the handle. And I started to feel bad. Mom and Dad sounded so worried about Cassie. If I went out the house, they'd be so worried about me too.

Maybe I shouldn't go out.

Maybe I should just wait inside.

I started to lower my hand and walk back upstairs when I saw something through the window down the street.

It was Cassie. She was running down the street, heading right back toward the house.

When I saw the snow bouncing up from her feet, I just wanted to go out there and run with her. 'Cause it wasn't fair. It wasn't fair that Cassie could run in the snow but I couldn't. I was eight. I was old enough to look after myself.

Besides. If I went out there and came back with Cassie, maybe Mom and Dad would see what a hero I was.

Maybe they'd see just how big and strong I was for saving my sister from the "chaos" and they'd let me go to Manhattan on my own or with my friends when I wanted after that. They'd let me get ice cream and play in Central Park. I'd feel all grown up.

So I lowered the handle of the front door and stepped out into the snow.

The snow felt so nice and cold against my skin. I heard it crunching under my feet. It was so bright to look at. And when I stuck my tongue out, it tasted like the freshest ice pop I'd ever eaten.

I didn't even close the door.

I just walked out into the street.

It was so quiet. The only sounds I could hear were my own footsteps, and Cassie getting closer.

I saw her running towards me. Lifted my hands. Jumped up and waved.

I expected her to look happy to see me. To smile at me. Cassie always smiled at me. Even though she picked on me sometimes, called me big ears, she always smiled at me.

But she didn't smile at me this time.

She waved her hands back.

"Get inside!" she shouted. "Get the hell inside!"

I didn't understand. I couldn't figure out why Cassie wasn't happy to see me. We always talked about how cool the ULTRAs were, how cool it'd be to be one. How we didn't think they were as bad as the people on the news and the TV made out.

Cassie told me stories about the ULTRAs. She read them to me before I went to sleep.

So why was she so scared right now?

"Get inside, Kyle!"

"What..."

I started to speak when I saw it.

A flash in the sky.

And then, right above me, just like that, they were there.

I stared up at them. Felt my jaw lower, the snow dripping into my mouth.

I'd seen them on the TV. I'd seen them on the internet and in the movies.

But I'd never seen them for real.

Saint and Orion were above me. Saint was dressed in that silver armor of his, with the metal mask over his face. He looked like a knight, but a scary one. I didn't like him, not as much as Orion.

Orion was dressed in that cool black outfit with the planet on his chest, the stars all around it. He looked cool. Even though people said the ULTRAs were bad, I thought he looked really cool.

I wanted to be like Orion when I was older. Only someone people liked instead of hated.

I watched them like I was looking at a movie. I could hear Cassie's shouts getting louder. Hear them getting closer. I thought I heard Mom and Dad shout, too.

I saw them shooting through the sky faster than my eyes could see. I saw them disappear. Saw them hover around one another like they were dancing, like the best wrestling match ever. I wanted to see them in the ring. I wanted to see who'd win if they were in WWE. I'd always wanted to go watch a wrestling match.

But right now, I was seeing a bigger one than ever.

Cassie kept on running towards me, but I couldn't look away from the battle in the sky.

Saint pummeled his fist into Orion's face.

But Orion dodged it.

Threw Saint down to the road below.

Sent me tumbling from my feet.

"It's over, Saint," Orion said, his voice strong and booming. "This ends. This ends right now."

Saint stood up. He looked broken. His legs wobbled around. He didn't look like an ULTRA. Not anymore. "Maybe it is," Saint said.

He lifted his hands and something happened.

A light sparked from Saint's chest. I felt the ground begin to shake. Felt this weird tingling up the back of my neck like I'd never felt before. The sky went black. The wind became strong, cold. Flames spurted from the middle of Saint's armor. A light shone from his chest.

"Come on then," Saint said. "End it. End it all."

Orion hovered there for a moment. He hovered there and stared at Saint.

And then he flew down at him.

"Good-bye, old sport," Saint said.

Cassie's fingertips reached mine.

"We need to—"

I didn't see what caused the bright light in the sky.

I didn't see it, but whatever it was knocked me to the road. I tasted metal in my mouth. I couldn't hear anything but ringing in my ears and couldn't see anything but light.

I felt electricity tingling through my body.

Tingling faster, faster...

When the light faded, I still couldn't hear properly. But I could see things. I could see that Saint and Orion were gone. I could see that there were flames burning in the middle of my street and that the roofs had blown off houses. I could see people opening their curtains, looking to see what'd happened.

And I could see Mom and Dad too. They were standing over me. But they didn't look happy.

They were crying.

I could feel Cassie's hand in mine. So I squeezed it. I squeezed it hard, to try and get her to move off me 'cause she was older than me so she was hurting me.

But Cassie didn't move.

She didn't squeeze back.

My sister—my favorite person in the world—never squeezed back again.

Eight years later...

I WALKED past the broken glass, past the fragments of sink and mirror all over the floor. I kept my eyes ahead. I didn't want to look around. Didn't want to see the chaos the gunmen had caused.

I just had to keep moving.

I just had to get out.

I stepped towards the exit of the restroom. Looked to the left. Clear. Then to the right. Totally clear.

"Please," I mumbled, my lips quivering. "Please."

And then I walked as quickly as I could over to those stairs.

When I reached them, adrenaline spinning through my body, I was pleasantly surprised to see the door at the bottom of the stairs open. The exit. Nobody was guarding it. My way out was right ahead.

I went to take a step when I felt something behind me.

Felt... like I was being watched.

I turned around, and every muscle in my body gave in.

One of the gunmen stood opposite. He was looking right into my eyes. Smiling.

His gun was pointed right at my chest.

"Sweet dreams, kid."

I squeezed my eyes shut and held my breath.

The gunman pulled the trigger.

This might seem like the ending to a story. It might seem like one of those dark conclusions, like one of those arty films that leave you with a bitter taste in your mouth.

But really, that moment is where my story began. Where things... well, changed. Forever.

But before that, there're a few things you need to understand about me.

Let's take it back a little...

2

It was safe to say I'd been afraid a few times in my life. But nothing quite like this.

The smell of sweat was strong in the changing rooms. Honestly, just a little whiff of it was enough to bring the taste of stomach acid to my mouth, make me want to heave. All around me, fellow sixteen-year-old boys getting changed, ready for the big traditional celebratory football game that marked the end of the season. A great way to unite the school year as it came to a close, the principal said. A celebration of friendships that went beyond jocks and geeks.

Unfortunately, the principal was a jock. He wanted this "celebration" for the same reason that every other meathead in the year wanted it.

To make fun of skinny little runts like me.

Oh, in front of girls, too.

A lot of girls.

The chatter of the changing room made my head spin. I kept on figuring out ways I could get out of this match. I thought about ringing in sick, but my mom would never let me get away with it. I considered hiding. But then if somebody found me, I'd just be known as that kid who hid on the day of the game, thus etching my place right near the top of the Staten Island High School Wuss Leaderboards for eternity. I'd never get a girlfriend. I'd never be popular.

Hell, I wouldn't be anyway, but that would only go to confirm it.

"Dunno why you get yourself in such a state, man."

I turned around and saw Damon looking at me. He was dressed in a furry lion costume. He didn't have the head on yet, and he didn't really need to, in truth. His curly brown locks hung over his ears like a mane. He had a little bear-type thing on his chin, which he desperately needed to start shaving ASAP. He was bigger than me, which meant that although he was hopeless at football, he was better built to take a few hits. I was short and scrawny. I was literally opposite to the football build.

But yeah. A lion costume for the game looked as ridiculous as it sounds.

Damon was my best friend. He'd been my best friend since elementary school. We both had something in common—we were losers, basically. We were the kind of kids who just attracted each other like a magnetic force when we started school; like we already knew we weren't gonna get anywhere with the popular kids, so we kind of just settled for each other.

But that was pretty harsh on Damon. He was loyal. He was a laugh. And I loved having him as a best friend.

One problem. He didn't give a damn about making a fool of himself.

Like dressing up as a lion for the game.

No one dressed up as a lion for the game.

Damon punched me in the arm. Probably not as hard as it felt, in truth, but I was a skinny thing so even the lightest tap was enough to cripple me.

"It's all just a big joke, remember?"

"It is to you. You're dressed as Mufasa."

"Well, maybe you should've brought a tight little Simba costume along with you, hmm?"

He started tickling the back of my neck with his lion fur. I could see a few of the other boys looking over at us, shaking their heads. You know, the muscular, well-built ones who would actually stand a chance at being real men someday? The ones I had literally zero chance of ever being like? Yeah. Those. We all know 'em. Like a different species in themselves. A better species.

"Come on, man. Just lighten up."

I held my breath as I walked by Damon's side out into the warm early summer air. It was a decent day, which wasn't a good thing. It meant the girls would be out to watch us all. At least if it'd been raining like hell, there'd be an excuse for them to not come along and embrace our misery.

Besides, I was wearing short shorts. I felt like I was naked.

This was serious code red level shit.

I needed to do something to get out of this.

"It's hard to lighten up when you're built like a skeleton with skin," I said.

"Hey, just think. All the girls'll be there to watch us."

My stomach turned. "Wonderful."

"And Ellicia will be there."

My stomach turned even more. "Right."

I didn't know what else to say about Ellicia Williams other than, well, she was gorgeous. And funny. And out of my league. And, oh, moderately cool, too, which made her infinitely less attainable.

"Right? All you can say is 'right'?"

I shrugged as I made that torturous walk towards the field. With the rest of the boys leading the way, the muscular ones, it felt like I was being led to my death. "Dunno why it matters."

"Man, it's obvious how damned much you love Ellicia."

I felt my cheeks flushing. "Keep your voice down."

"Why? Everyone knows—"

"Which is fine," I said. "I'd just... I'd just rather not right now, okay?"

"So you're admitting it?"

"Admitting what?"

"That you like Ell—"

"I didn't say that!"

"You kinda said that."

"Damon, please."

Damon held his lion paws up. He was literally the only person in the school year of four-hundred taking advantage of the fancy dress rule. "Hey. I'm just saying. She's cute, and she's not been snapped up by one of Mike's boys yet. She's about to get smoking hot, so I say get in there before she does. Because when she does, you really won't have a chance. No offense."

"None taken."

Damon's words were all well and good. I could see he was just looking out for me, in his annoying, beyond weird way.

But the truth was, I was never getting a girl like Ellicia. I was never getting a girl.

I wasn't the kind of guy girls went for. I didn't even know how to *talk* to a girl, for heaven's sakes.

Besides, the fact that Damon was so sure Ellicia would be at the game wasn't reassuring in any way, shape or form.

It was damned terrifying.

I reached the field. I could hear the crowd starting to applaud. Under my arm, I held my helmet. I went to snap it on right away.

"Why you putting that on already?"

"'Cause I don't want anyone to recognize me."

"Man, they won't recognize you. Nobody's looking at you."

"Yes, but they might be looking at the only frigging *lion* this side of the Bronx Zoo!"

I went to pull my helmet on when I saw Mike Beacon looking right at me.

I couldn't believe it. I seriously thought he'd let it go, just for this one day. That he'd be too focused on impressing his football mates, the crowd of girls, to give a hell about me.

But there he was. Muscular. Short blond hair. Bright blue eyes. Standing at the top of the hill just before the field. Staring at me. Smile on his face.

I felt my guts turn to mush right then.

But even more so when I saw Ellicia standing right by the side of the field.

Also looking right at me.

"Keep moving, squirt."

I felt someone push into my back.

"Come on, Kyle. Field is straight ahead."

I couldn't move. My legs were locked. I literally could not take a step closer to that field, no matter how hard I tried.

I was stuck. Stuck in the gaze of Mike Beacon, the guy who'd made my school years a misery on nearly a daily basis.

And the gaze of Ellicia.

I saw her chocolate brown hair swaying in the breeze. I saw those thick-rimmed glasses perched on the end of her nose, which actually made her look hella hotter. I saw her sparkling blue eyes that always made me feel fuzzy inside, ever since the day I'd first met her.

I saw her, and I knew there was only one thing for me to do.

I turned around, and I ran.

I saw the confused looks of the people behind me in line as I powered past them. I heard voices calling out, asking what the hell I was doing.

I said the only words I knew would get me out of a situation like this.

"Restroom!" I shouted, clutching onto my stomach. "I need —I need the restroom."

I heard the laughter erupting but knew it wouldn't matter. I had my helmet on. Nobody knew who I was.

"Restroom!" I said, trying to work my way around more people. "Seriously need it. Scuse me. Thanks. Thanks."

I kept on going with no regard for the stupidity of what I was doing until I reached the changing room restroom and slammed the door shut.

I pulled off my helmet. Let out some deep breaths. "Shit," I muttered. "Shit, shit, shit." I was trapped in here now. Trapped until the game started, at least. Hopefully, the game would be so good that I'd be forgotten. Hopefully, none of the students would even notice I was gone.

I sat down on the toilet. Waited.

And then I heard a knock on the door.

I went still. Completely still. I didn't say a word. If I just stayed quiet, I could—

"Kyle, are you in there?"

I could recognize the voice. Mr. Preacher, the history teacher. Fortunately, he was old and senile, so he wouldn't even care about the football, let alone the fact that I was on the loo. I was one of his favorites. Not like he was going to publicly shame me.

"Kyle? Are you—"

"Yes," I shouted. "Yes, I... I've got the squirts, sir. Can't take part in the game. Sir."

I thought I heard sniggering. But then... no. Mr. Preacher couldn't be sniggering. He never sniggered at anything.

I waited a few seconds. Mr. Preacher didn't say anything else. It was totally silent outside. On the field, I could hear the cheers kicking in. The game must be starting. Now was my chance.

I stood up. Unlocked the restroom door.

It was only when I turned the handle that I realized two things.

One, how had Mr. Preacher known that it was me, Kyle, in the restroom?

And two...

Mike Beacon was fire at impressions.

I heard the laughter erupt when I opened the restroom door. Saw the cameras flash. Hell, even Damon was there, lion head in his arms, laughing along with the rest of this crowd.

Mike Beacon stood right at the front of the group. He was squatted down, straining. "I've got the squirts, sir!" he said, in a mock voice that was, admittedly, remarkably like my own. "Sir, I've got the squirts!"

I felt like on the embarrassment-o-meter, I'd hit the peak right there. I felt like nothing would ever top this. This was my OK Computer, and nothing I did after this would ever come close, even though there'd be some damned fine contenders. Nothing.

And then I saw Ellicia staring at me, smile on her face, and I realized I was wrong about that peak.

3

"**M**an, seriously. You should've seen it. It was like, straight dope. The straightest, dopiest thing I've ever seen."

I listened to Damon's ninety-third retelling of the events of earlier that day and wished I could be anywhere but here.

Only here was the one place I actually enjoyed being. With my friends.

What a wonderful life I had.

"So did you legit shit yourself in front of the whole school?" Avi asked.

"No, I didn't legit shit myself."

"Just fake-shitted himself," Damon corrected. He fiddled around with his phone. "Anyway, should be on YouTube by now."

"I really don't think anyone will have actually gone ahead and uploaded it to—"

"Here it is!"

"Oh. Okay. Maybe the world really has gone completely down the drain."

I listened to Damon and Avi laugh as they watched me open

that door. As they listened to me mutter those, "I've got the squirts!" words. They even laughed at Mike Beacon's impressions, which was funny because they couldn't stand the guy just as much as me.

I tried to focus on Fallout 4. My hands were clammy. The thought of takeaway pizza that Damon had ordered didn't exactly feel too appealing. My guts were still struggling to cope with the levels of embarrassment my body had forced upon them. Didn't help that Avi's food reeked of pizza. Always. Even when there was no pizza in sight. I swore he wore pizza spray or something.

"Oh, man," Avi said. He shook his head. Avi was a quite chubby guy with a big black beard and glasses. He didn't go to my school—thank the Lord. I loved the guy. Straight up guy and as honest a friend as you could wish for.

But damn, he made Damon look cool.

"You're gonna have to get a grip of that, Damon," Avi said. "Wouldn't wanna lose it."

"You really would want to lose it," I said, trying to keep my bleary-eyed focus on Avi's PlayStation 4.

"No worries if we do lose it," Damon said. "There's already hundreds of videos of it all over the net."

"Holy smokes," Avi said, leaning over and grabbing the controller off me. "You're internet famous, Kyle. That ain't anything we can boast about. Unless you count the time Mick Drake set fire to my jeans."

"I'd rather not count either," I said.

"Oh, lighten up, man. Nobody'll remember it this time tomorrow."

"You really think so?"

Avi started up Fallout 4 again. He adjusted his glasses. "Actually, no. I lied. Everyone will remember it this time next year, let alone tomorrow."

"Wow. Thanks."

"You know how I am. Honest as they get."

I leaned back and watched Avi on Fallout 4. Damon and I chatted about a few things—new computing rigs we wanted to get installed, the state of iOS14 and the new security features the government was *still* trying to push through congress, some world event conspiracy stuff that always intrigued Damon. But we couldn't speak for long without Damon bursting out laughing again, pulling that impression Mike Beacon did.

It annoyed me at first. And I kind of wanted to put Damon straight. He'd done plenty of similarly stupid crap in his time at school, only problem was, he was so oblivious of social norms that he genuinely didn't care.

But as much as I wanted to stand up for myself, I knew that I couldn't. Because it was just who I was. I was the sixteen-year-old freak who shat himself before the football game. That wasn't contrary to anything else I'd done before. I was viewed as a bit of a nerd, I knew that. I didn't exactly do many nerdy things, in all truth. My hair was short, dark, fairly trendy, I thought. I didn't wear glasses—not that glasses were a bad thing. I dressed as well as the next guy, I thought.

The difference between the average popular kid and me? I didn't stand up for myself. I was scared of standing up for myself.

Hell. I'd go as far as saying I was scared of other people.

That's what made me a nerd.

That's what made me the antithesis to the social butterfly.

And that's just who I was.

"Seriously, though, dude," Damon said as he sipped back on his Coca-Cola. "It's about time you started being a man and told Ellicia how you really feel."

I felt my skin tingle with cold.

"Oh, he's still stanning on that Ellicia chick?" Avi asked.

"Stanning?" I asked.

"Yeah, y'know. Eminem. Stan. Obsessing. It's a hip-hop thing."

"Right. 'Cause you're so hip hop."

"Don't ever say hip hop like that again."

"Right. Sure. Got it."

"But seriously," Avi asked. "Known her since sixth grade and you still haven't come clean with Ellicia?"

I was both relieved at being off the me fake-shitting myself conversation and annoyed that the conversation had veered into the territory of the girl I'd been mad about since I first laid eyes on her. "I dunno. I'll get round to it. Not like there's a rush."

"Man, there's always a rush," Avi said.

"That's what I've been tellin' him for ages. She's blossoming. She's gonna be straight fire soon. How you gonna feel when she's straight fire and you missed out on her while she's still all humble?"

I kind of got Damon's point. But it irritated me to hear anyone using the term "straight fire," especially my best friend.

"Anyway," Avi said. "Probably doesn't matter much anymore. Not after you full on shat yourself."

"I didn't—"

"Sorry, sorry. After you fake shat yourself. But point stands. Doesn't matter. She's not gonna touch you with a bargepole anymore."

I felt my stomach sink. I wasn't sure I could feel much lower about my self-esteem. "Thanks for the pep talk."

Avi turned. Winked. "Not a problem, Skids."

I bit my tongue through Avi's nickname and tried not to flip.

"When have you ever been such a ladies' man, anyway?" I asked. It wasn't exactly me flipping—me flipping just didn't happen. But it was as close as I was going to get.

"Actually," Avi said, hitting pause. He leaned over. Held his phone out. "I've been chattin' to a girl lately."

Damon's jaw dropped. "You've been *chatting* to a girl?"

Avi grinned and nodded. "Hell yeah. We've been getting close a few weeks now. Here she is."

Avi held out his phone. I felt bad for expecting to see someone less-than-attractive, or maybe even someone out of a video game.

But instead, I saw a... genuinely attractive female human being.

"Whaddya think?" Avi asked.

"This... this isn't a wind-up?" I asked.

Avi shook his head. "Ain't no wind-up."

"And she's actually *met* you?"

"We've Facebook met."

"Facebook met?"

"We've chatted on Facebook."

"So you haven't *actually* met?"

"We're in the process of meeting, man. Besides, it's closer than any of you two's got to any action."

He put his phone away. Me nor Damon couldn't exactly argue.

As I watched Avi return to his game, I couldn't shake that minuscule irritation once again. A bad kind of irritation. But I felt something like jealousy. Jealousy that my friend, who I was no more nerdy than, less so if anything, had been chatting to a girl.

"How'd that come about?" I asked.

"Miri? Oh, I just saw her on Instagram. Thought she was cute. We got chatting."

"Wait," I said, shaking my head. "Am I in some alternate reality? You followed a girl on Instagram who you thought was cute and you... you got chatting?"

"I just believed in myself, man. Believe in yourself some more. Girls like that. Everyone likes that. When you believe, you can do anything."

"Profound."

"Plus, I read a hell of a lot of dating blogs."

"Ah. That makes more sense."

"And I used some foolproof chat up lines from the top reviewed online dating guide on Goodreads."

"Again. Making much more sense. I'd like to see you use that in person."

"4.6 stars, man. 4.6 stars out of 5. Da-ting book of the year."

Again, I kind of felt cheated that I hadn't thought to read a book like that myself. Maybe Avi was right. Maybe I did just need to loosen up, believe in myself a little more.

I was mulling over the thought of asking Ellicia out—as impossible as that was—when my phone buzzed.

I read the message. And as I read it, I felt sicker—somehow —than I had for the entire day.

"You okay, dude?" Damon asked. "Gone pale."

I put the phone down. Swallowed a lump in my throat. "Yeah, I..." I stood up. Headed toward Avi's door.

"Skids?" Avi asked. "Where you headed?"

I got ready to leave Avi's house, the truth of the message sending nerves tingling through my stomach. "Sorry, guys. It's been fun. But there's somewhere I need to be right now."

"Can't it wait?"

I wished it could.

4

W hen I walked into my Staten Island home, I knew right away what I was going to face.

The walls of the hallway were dark, and the wallpaper was curling at the edges. As I walked past them, I tried not to look at the photographs pinned up to the wall. Some people liked to be reminded of times they'd once had. Of the things they'd lost. But I didn't. I didn't like being reminded of the day my parents' lives tore apart. The day that changed my life, forever.

I could hear crying in the kitchen. Mumbling. I knew without seeing that it was Mom. I held my breath as I pushed open the kitchen door. It wasn't that I didn't know what I was going to face. Nobody could accuse me of not being prepared.

But it never got easier.

Grief never got easier.

That was something I had come to understand in my sixteen mostly miserable years on this planet.

Mom was on her knees. She was sweeping something from the kitchen floor. It looked like the remnants of a smashed dinner plate. Tears were streaming down her cheeks.

"Mom?"

She looked up. Stopped sweeping right away. She forced a smile, quickly wiped the tears from her eyes as if it'd cover up the fact she'd been crying effectively. Her light brown hair hung limply by the sides of her head. She looked older, more wrinkled, every time I saw her. Her skin was pale like she desperately needed a holiday. She never dressed up—right now she was in gray joggers and a white T-shirt, which had turned a shade yellow. "Kyle," she said. "He's... He's... I can't..."

"Where is he?"

"In the living room," Mom whispered. "I just don't think I can watch him do this anymore. I don't think I can handle it."

I felt my stomach sinking when I heard the upset in Mom's voice. I walked over to her. Hugged her. It felt nice when she hugged me. The smell of her hair always took me back right to my earliest memory, when she was holding me in her arms, rocking me from side to side.

"Sorry to bring you home from your friends."

"It's okay. We were pretty much done anyway."

"You always say that."

"What?"

"You always say that. You were pretty much done. Kyle, I'm... I'm sorry. I just don't know how to handle him when he's like this. You're the only person who can get through to him."

I pulled back from my mom's hug. Wiped her salty tears from my face. I smiled at her. "Don't worry. I've got it."

"You're a good boy, Kyle. A good boy."

I turned around and nodded. She was right about that.

Just a pity the "good boys" didn't get anywhere in life.

I walked up to the living room door. Part of me just wanted to turn around and run away. Mom might think I was the only person who could deal with Dad when he was upset, but the truth was, I was just winging it too. I didn't really know what to say. Didn't really know what I was doing.

I just felt like I should be there.

Because I guess, I felt weirdly responsible for his misery.

I let out that deep breath and lowered the handle.

My dad was sat in the corner of the room. To the everyday bystander, it looked like he was just sitting there, having a rest.

But I knew my dad. And I knew he was having what Mom called an "event."

An "event" that he'd been having ever since The Great Blast killed my sister.

"Dad?"

He looked up. He was usually bald, although his shaven head was growing pretty long. His beard was wispy and gray. His eyes were sunken, dark underneath. His smile was flat. Empty.

Dad didn't look healthy. But he hadn't looked healthy for eight years.

To say that this was the dad I knew wasn't an easy thing to admit.

"You should be out with your friends," Dad said.

I nodded. Walked over to him. "We finished. I—"

"Did your mom tell you to come speak to me?"

I paused. "No," I said. "I just got back and saw the kitchen in a state. Figured something must've happened."

Dad tutted. Shook his head. "You've always been an awful liar, son."

I sat beside my dad. "I'll take that as a compliment."

We sat there in silence for a few minutes. Stared across the room at the television, which wasn't switched on. One of the photographs on the fireplace caught my eye. One of Dad with Cassie on his shoulders at some summer fair. The photograph had faded a little in the sunlight. But I knew there were plenty other photographs Dad could switch it with if he needed another to look at; to remind himself.

I tried not to remind myself too often. But in moments like these, I couldn't deny the wandering of my mind. The wandering to a time that seemed an eternity ago; a time that already filled the history lessons even though it only ended when I was eight.

Dad had been this way ever since The Great Blast. Some people doubted The Great Blast. Some people questioned whether it was really as deadly and terrifying as the teachers and the New York old-timers made it out to be.

But it was. Because I'd seen it.

I'd watched it take my fourteen-year-old sister away.

Like Hiroshima and Nagasaki before it, The Great Blast was a bittersweet event. It marked the end of the Era of the ULTRAs. Now let me educate you on ULTRAs a little. ULTRAs were supposed to be the future. The First World War was a turning point for the planet. It fast became clear that full armies were not a sustainable way to fight. There was too much damage. Too much collateral. Too many scars. So the leaders of the world got to work on the ultimate arms race: a way to find an alternative to conventional warfare.

It took time. There were harrowing human experiments by the Nazis. Nuclear explosions. There was the Cold War, the information war, counter-terrorism and drone strikes. But nothing was right for the purpose. Nothing replaced the old-fashioned methods of conflict that'd spanned since the beginning of time. It was still just a human and a weapon of some form or other.

Until the discovery of the ULTRAs.

Nobody knew exactly how the ULTRAs came about. Not publicly, anyway. Just that fifteen years ago, the United States government unveiled their very first creation. Some people said they were modified humans. Others said they were the products of genetic experiments. Nobody really minded as long as they protected the planet.

The powers of the ULTRAs varied. Some had just the one —the ability to fly, or the ability to run at super-speed. Others had tricks of the mind, like the power of super-thought, and the ability to crack codes that not even the best computers could manage.

There were rare ones, too. ULTRAs that had multiple abilities. Telekinesis. Teleportation.

The most well known of those with multiple abilities?

Saint and Orion.

Of course, they weren't called ULTRAs then. ULTRA by its definition means extremist, something that they were only regarded as four years after the introduction of Alpha.

Originally? They were simply known as Heroes.

And they were going to change the world.

They did just that.

Only not in the way the government planned.

The first few Heroes went down without a hitch. There was a reduction in military spending because of them. Police presence was less required. People seemed safer on the streets. Those four years between Alpha's introduction and the change from Heroes to ULTRAs were reportedly some of the most blissful in human existence.

Then some of the Heroes decided they wanted more than just to gate-keep the planet.

As with everything powerful, some of the power started getting to the Heroes' heads. After a series of devastating scuffles within the ranks, one Hero rose to the top of the villainous food chain: Saint.

Saint led three years of terror. He launched attacks on cities.

He terrorized people for fun. His goal? Complete control of the planet. Complete superiority over humans.

He wanted humans to fear him. And he wanted humans to serve him.

He didn't want Heroes to be the new gods. He wanted Heroes to be the new humans.

The humans? They were just the cattle underneath.

It didn't help that he had multiple abilities. That he was the most powerful ULTRA in existence.

With the Heroes becoming ULTRAs by definition, the tables turned. ULTRAs of all kinds were hunted down by government forces. Military spending was ramped right back up again to levels it'd never before reached. Curfews were in place. Humanity faced near certain extinction as more and more ULTRAs converted to Saint's ways.

All of them except Orion.

Orion was different. He was powerful, just like Saint, which was remarkable in itself, leading many to assume he was a product of severe government experimentation. Instead of turning to the side of Saint, he fought for what he believed in. Even though the government demanded he back down, he kept on hunting Saint's people, desperate to force them into oblivion.

And he did. After three dark years, leaving Saint and Orion the last two known ULTRAs standing, Orion succeeded. He defeated Saint.

But in the end, it wasn't the government demands that destroyed the last of the ULTRAs. It was themselves.

Saint triggered something just before Orion pounded into him, with all the power he had in turn. Between them, they triggered an ultimate power source within, something people were still trying to explain to this day. Pure Hero power.

And that caused The Great Blast.

The event that ended the Era of the ULTRAs.

The explosion that killed one million New Yorkers.

The explosion that ripped through my Staten Island neighborhood. That I, somehow, survived.

That my sister, Cassie, died in.

Where my father's descent into depression began.

There was something weird about The Great Blast, admittedly. Nobody knew why some survived and some didn't. It wasn't just any old explosion—it was a pure collision of ULTRA abilities.

Whatever it was, it marked the end. The end of an era that started with such hope. Hope of a new army. Hope of a new police. Hope of a new deterrent against all the world's evils.

After the blast, Mom always wanted to move from Sherman Avenue. To get a fresh start. Our place was one of the lucky ones that stayed standing, despite everything.

But Dad couldn't move on. He'd never even cleared out Cassie's room.

To this day, I still hadn't walked into that room. It gave me the creeps even thinking about it. Like there were ghosts of a dark past waiting in there for me, and if I opened that door, I'd let them out all over again.

"I'm here for you, Dad," I said. "Don't... don't ever forget that. I'm here for you."

Dad didn't say anything in response to me. And I knew why.

Dad didn't care that I was here for him.

Because what could I do?

What could a weak-ass little pussy who fake-shat himself to get out of a game of football do to ease his grief?

What could a failure like me do?

I sat there in silence, Dad silent by my side.

As I stared at the photograph of Cassie, I thought back to the final time I'd seen her.

Running out into the street to try and save her when Mom and Dad were so worried.

Trying to be the hero.

Failing.

I'd never tried to be the hero since that day. Never.

Because I saw what being the hero did to people.

I saw what Orion trying to be the hero did to one million New Yorkers, to their families.

Heroes were overrated. The world didn't need them messing things up. Not again.

At least, that's what I thought.

5

Daniel Septer sat in his bedroom and listened to the arguments downstairs.

He was so used to hearing conflict between his mom and his stepdad, Garth, that it was beginning to lose all meaning. Outside, in the darkness of night, Daniel heard the rain rattling against the window, the wind shaking it. He'd never enjoyed the darkness. Always found it so spooky, so creepy.

That's probably why Garth didn't like him, either. Too soft to be a son of his. Too weak.

The voices downstairs got louder. Daniel felt the tension in his stomach tingling away. The hairs on the back of his neck stood on end. He could smell food cooking; a meal for the pair of them that hadn't worked out. Maybe Mom cooked something for Garth, and he didn't appreciate it. Or maybe Mom made an offhand comment about something Garth made, and he didn't take too nicely. There was always something between them. Some sticking point, something to make them argue. It'd been that way ever since they met three years ago.

Daniel didn't ever step in or intervene. Because he'd heard how loud Garth could shout. He'd heard how loud it got before a sudden silence kicked in and the pair of them went quiet, completely quiet.

And he didn't like to think about what happened when it went quiet. *Why* it went quiet.

So he just sat in his bedroom on his creaky single bed and played his video games.

Daniel never wanted to be this way. He always wanted to be strong; he still *wanted* to be strong. But he'd never had the courage to stand up to anyone, whether it be at school or at home. It'd been that way since he lost his dad in The Great Blast. Mom said that's what'd made him weak; Garth just told her Daniel was weak from birth. That some kids were just wired up that way. Wired up wrong.

But not his kid. No kid of his.

Daniel carried on pounding away on the controller, hoping the sounds of the rain and the wind would cover up the sounds of the shouts, when he heard a high-pitched scream.

Daniel felt something then. Felt something unfamiliar. Something he had felt at some stage in his life, but something he couldn't pinpoint.

He knew it was his mom's scream he heard.

And that she sounded in pain. In danger.

He wanted to go down there. Check she was okay.

But even more than that, Daniel knew he couldn't go downstairs because Garth was down there, and he was too weak to stand up to Garth, too weak to tell him to—

Another scream.

This one louder.

Daniel felt that sensation inside again, and he wanted to do something. He wanted to react. He hadn't felt this way since he lost his dad. He remembered it now. Remembered that tingling feeling as the windows in the flats either side of him caved in.

He remembered the sounds of the screams all around him, the feel of the explosion blast into his body.

He remembered that tingling feeling and remembered his dad's body going limp.

And it made him angry.

It made him so...

The feeling overwhelmed him, filled every inch of his body... and then he was standing in the middle of the kitchen with Garth and Mom.

Daniel stood there a few seconds. His heart pounded. He couldn't understand how he was here. One second, he was in his bedroom. Now, he was downstairs with them.

He couldn't be down here. This couldn't be possible. It couldn't—

"What the hell are you doing down here, boy?"

Daniel heard Garth's voice and felt a shiver creep up the back of his neck.

He turned around, looked over towards the oven and the counters, and he saw them.

Garth was standing, but Mom was on her knees. She was crying. Holding her stomach, like she was in pain.

There was something in Garth's eyes. Redness. His sleeves were rolled up.

"I asked you a question, squirt. What the hell are you doing down here?"

Daniel wanted to go back to his room. To run away from these people he barely recognized as his mom and his stepdad.

But he felt that tingling sensation grow stronger.

He felt that *urge* to do something building inside.

That memory of his dad dying beside him. The dad who should be here right now, making Mom happy.

Not this man.

"Go... go to your room, Daniel," Mom said. She barely spat the words out. "It's—It's okay. It's okay."

Daniel looked around the kitchen. Over into the dining room. He saw a card and wrapping paper on the table. On the floor, a shirt. It was ripped.

And suddenly reality dawned on Daniel. It was Garth's birthday. Mom bought him a shirt. A shirt he didn't like.

And he was punishing her for it.

Garth was punishing Daniel's mom because he didn't like the shirt she bought him.

Daniel turned around, and he saw Garth walking towards him.

"Garth, no!"

"I told you to go upstairs," Garth said.

Daniel saw the redness building in Garth's eyes. He saw his fist tensing. He could feel in the air that Garth had wanted to do this for a long time. He'd been waiting for the right moment, for the right opportunity.

This was it.

This was his moment.

"But seeing as you're stayin'," Garth said, squaring right up to Daniel, towering over him, "might as well teach you a few manners."

"Garth, please!"

Garth pulled back his fist.

Hurtled it toward Daniel's face.

Daniel felt that anger, that tingling, within. And he felt something leave his body. An energy, that was the only way he could describe it.

It took him a few seconds to realize what was happening.

But then he saw the confused look on Garth's face.

He saw his fist stuck inches from Daniel's nose.

Just stuck there in mid-air.

It took Daniel by surprise. He couldn't understand. Couldn't get his head around it. But deep down, he got that *he* was doing this somehow. He was stopping Garth's fist, midair. He was using that tingling feeling—that same tingling he'd felt on the day of The Great Blast—and he was stopping Garth from punching him.

"What the—" Garth started.

He didn't finish.

Daniel used that tingling feeling, used that anger, to turn Garth's fist around.

Turn it so it was pointing at his own nose.

He bit his lip. Tasted blood at the back of his throat.

But in his mind, he heard the screams of his mom.

He saw the sadness in her eyes.

He saw that shirt, ripped, on the floor.

And he used his mind to crack Garth's fist into his own face.

The force of the impact knocked Garth back. He flew across the room, slammed against the cupboards, hit the floor.

And Daniel knew he should stop. He knew he should run away and hide because whatever this was, it was dangerous. Whatever this was, it was getting him into trouble.

But instead, he kept on tensing.

Kept on using his mind, his anger, to swing Garth's fist against his own face.

To beat himself right there on the floor, nothing he could do about it.

He heard Garth begging him to stop. He heard Mom asking him to give in, too. To quit whatever he was doing.

But Daniel kept on going.

He kept on going because the anger was turning into excitement.

He kept on going because for so long he'd wanted to do this, to stand up to someone, to beat the bully.

He kept on going because for the first time in his life, he felt strong.

He didn't know how long exactly he kept going. But when he stopped, Garth was still. Completely still.

He took a deep breath. Walked over to his mom. Reached down and hugged her.

"We're going to be okay now, Mom," he said, holding her close. "Everything's going to be okay now."

Blood trickled across the kitchen floor.

Daniel felt alive.

[6]

I knew I was probably a little over-ambitious when I planned on not being noticed at school after yesterday's fake-shit embarrassment.

When I felt something hit the back of my head as I sat in the middle of the geography classroom, I knew it'd be a long time before attention turned from me.

It was two o'clock, and the day was dragging like hell. It was sunny outside as summer progressed, which made me just want to get out into that sunlight more than anything. New York was funny like that. Winter was ridiculously cold, and then spring and summer came out of nowhere, bringing along droves of tourists, making every single classroom eternally sweaty.

I pulled against the front of my shirt and watched the clock as Mrs. Porter droned on and on about erosion and the ice caps and global warming and blah blah blah.

The sooner this day was over, the better.

I didn't want to look around, but I knew from the occasional sniggers and whispers that they were directed at me. I was the news of the day, it turned out. Everyone who didn't know about fake-shit-gate now *did* know, and there were variations of the story going round, like me running back to the toilets with poop trailing down my leg, me getting ready to kick the football only to squirt out a poop—yeah, a lot of poop related variants. Perhaps my favorite imaginative story was the one where apparently, I was pooping in the same loo as Mr. Preacher, my history teacher. That there was something weird going on between us. Even though Mr. Preacher's only link to this whole thing was Mike Beacon making an impression of his damned voice.

I wanted to dismiss the rumors. To expose them for their ridiculousness.

But I wasn't the kind of guy who stood up to people, so I had to just make do with laying as low as I possibly could and laughing off as best as I could.

I looked at the floor beside me. Saw there was a crumpled up note. That must've been what hit the side of my head. I could see some of Mike Beacon's friends at that side of the classroom, so I knew it must be something they'd done.

Unsure of whether to keep on ignoring them or not, I decided to reach down and pick the note up. I opened it.

I wished I hadn't.

It was a rather detailed, imaginative drawing of me, believe it or not. I was crouching down over a toilet, questionable substances squeezing out of my backside. Tears poured out of my eyes in a cartoonish manner.

A speech bubble: "I've got the squirts, sir! I've got the squirts!"

The weirdest part of all was the sketch of Mr. Preacher standing in front of me, his you-know-what in his hands. He sure looked like he was enjoying himself.

I heard the sniggers again and knew what Mike Beacon's friends were trying to do. They were spreading the rumors about Mr. Preacher, about me going crying to him, even though that wasn't what happened. I wanted to glare back at them.

Truth be told, I hadn't slept too well. Never did sleep too well when something went down with my parents. I'd spent 'til late just sitting beside my dad in the living room, waiting for him to come around and apologize to Mom.

When they finally went to bed at 2.a.m., I closed my eyes and disappeared into a four-hour sleep. A restless one at that.

"Kyle? Are you with us?"

Mrs. Porter. Shit.

"Um, I—"

"I hope it's global warming you're thinking so deeply about, young man," she said, in that sarcastic drone. She was a short woman, quite plump, with thick-rimmed glasses atop her bulbous nose.

I felt my cheeks getting warmer. Mrs. Porter wasn't the kind to take any prisoners. "Yeah. I was just, erm... I was thinking about how warm it is. For—for early summer. Whether that has anything to do with... with global, um, warming."

I heard a few sniggers around the class. Mrs. Porter narrowed her eyes. "Oh, that's interesting. 'Cause we finished talking about global warming a good half hour ago."

Shit. A Porter trap. A Porter trap I'd fallen right into.

"Sorry, miss," I said.

"Oh, don't apologize to me. Apologize to your classmates for holding up their lesson."

I nodded.

When I realized Mrs. Porter wasn't adding anything to her demands, I realized she was serious.

"Go on," she said. "Turn around to each and every one of your classmates, look them in the eyes and say sorry."

"Miss, I—"

"What's up, Kyle?" someone at the back of the class said. "Need another poop?"

The class filled with laughter. I felt my face heating up. I didn't know what to say or what to do, just that I wanted out of here.

"Stand up," Mrs. Porter said. "Look into each and every one of your classmates' eyes and say sorry."

"But I—"

"Just do it, Kyle."

I gritted my teeth. My heart pounded. I didn't want to do this. I just wanted to get out of this mess, one way or another. This was a nightmare. This was hell. I didn't think I could sink any lower than I already had. Evidently, I was wrong.

I pulled back my chair. Better to just get it over and done with.

I looked around at my classmates. Looked at each and every one of them. I saw them trying to hold in their laughter. Saw some of them staring at me like I was weird.

And then I saw Ellicia.

Her glasses were at the edge of her desk so I could see right into her eyes. Weird how different someone looked when they didn't have their glasses on. Ellicia looked amazing either way.

She wasn't smiling. She wasn't laughing. She was just looking at me differently to all the others. And I figured that was okay. If Ellicia was looking at me like she was, then nothing else mattered. Sure, she had to find what happened yesterday hilarious, but as long as she didn't mock me right now, everything was fine.

"I'm sorry," I said. "For—"

"Zip your fly up, Kyle, for hell's sakes!"

I heard the voice from the back of the class. From Harry Walker, one of Mike Beacon's best friends. And then I heard the class around him erupt into laughter.

No. I'd zipped my flies up. This was a joke. It had to be a...

When I looked down at the front of my pants, I saw it wasn't a joke.

My flies were unzipped.

My red, stripy boxer shorts were on show.

I listened to the chorus of laughter and felt my face burning to melting point. I looked around at everyone. Saw each and every one of them laughing, and I wished right then I could go full Carrie on them.

But when I saw Ellicia smiling, trying to hold back the laughter, a new feeling sparked inside me.

I felt upset. Like someone had converted my embarrassment into madness, into anger.

And then I felt a tingling sensation shoot up my body.

I squeezed my hands together.

Gritted my teeth.

And then I heard the blast.

The laughter disappeared. It turned into screams. A few yelps of shock.

I felt a breeze hit my face. My heart still pounded. I didn't know what'd happened.

Not until I looked to my right and saw the windows had smashed.

"Everybody outside!" Mrs. Porter shouted. She rushed over to the alarm and hit it. And I could sense the fear in the air. The panic. Gun crime was just something that happened in the modern world. The windows had smashed. Someone was here. Someone was on our campus. Something was happening.

I watched my classmates rush past me and felt like they were moving in slow motion, like everything around me was unfolding in slow motion.

I heard their screams, smelled their sweat, but I couldn't take my attention away from that moment.

That moment I'd felt the tingling in my body.

The upset.

The anger.

The moment I'd squeezed my fists together and heard the windows smash.

But more than anything, I couldn't focus on anything but the windows.

The glass wasn't inside the classroom.

The windows had smashed from the inside.

"Come on, Kyle," Mrs. Porter said. She put a hand on my back. "We'll deal with you later."

I stood still for a few seconds. Listened to the alarm ring through the school, the panic spread like wildfire to more of the classrooms.

And then I took a deep breath and followed the rest of the crowd out of the class, out of the school.

I didn't think much else about the incident in the classroom for the rest of the day. Mostly because I was just relieved to be able to leave school early.

It felt a bit surreal. Like something... weird had happened to me, sure. I felt a bit strange.

But nowhere near as strange as I was about to feel.

Nowhere as strange as what was ahead.

7

When Damon told me he was taking me somewhere to forget about the problems of the last two days, a soccer game was *not* what I was expecting.

"It'll be fun," Damon said, as we walked towards the Yankee Stadium to see New York City FC. The floodlights were bright. I could see other people walking towards the stadium entrance, hear the crowd inside with all their noise and... well, racket that I didn't enjoy, and wanted to steer far away from. The smell of dingy hotdog stands was strong in the air, making me want to hurl.

"How in any way, shape or form do you think I'd find this fun?"

"It's football," Damon said, grinning. He chewed down on some pink cotton candy. He was wearing a New York Yankees shirt that looked way too small for his bulbous belly, and his hair was swept back behind his ears in a way that I'd never seen him attempt before. "It's what manly men do."

"No," I said, trying to keep my cool, as impossible as that was. "This is *soccer*. It's not football."

"Football and soccer are the same things, right?"

"No. No, they aren't. Not unless you're British."

"I'm not British."

"Then this isn't a football game we're going to."

The realization clicked on Damon's face. His eyes widened. "Oh. So this... this *isn't* football?"

I shook my head and sighed. I wasn't in the mood for dicking around right now. "We shouldn't be here. We should... we should just go back."

Damon smacked my back. "No chance." He pushed me forward so I edged towards the turnstiles faster than I'd have liked.

"Damon, please—"

"Coming through!" Damon said. People glared at me as Damon nudged me past them. I tried to fight free of Damon, to run away from him, but before I knew it, I was at the turnstiles, the security guy glaring at me and asking for my ticket.

"Still want to back out?" Damon asked, a piece of cotton candy dangling from his chin.

I sighed. "I guess I don't have much of a choice."

We pushed our way inside the stadium. Truth be told, it was a lot more crowded than I thought soccer matches got. Soccer was kind of like football's weak cousin here in the States. It was big in Europe, and the rest of the world, but from what I gathered from... well, the people around me and online who had a moderate interest in sport, soccer was dull. Which I found hard to accept seeing as I couldn't think of anything duller than football.

We stepped out into the seating area. The field was massive and very green. The people around me all sipping their beers, eating their fast food... they just looked different to me right off the bat. Like they were supposed to be here; like they were comfortable here.

"Where we sat?" I asked Damon.

Damon shrugged. "I dunno."

"Well, why don't you have a look at the tickets and figure it out from there?"

Damon flipped his ticket over. Squinted at it, still chewing down on cotton candy, some of it trailing down the side of his mouth. "Row 35. Seat 122. So that should be..."

Both of us looked over to where we were supposed to be sitting.

For a moment, I was relieved to see those two empty seats. I just wanted to sit down and turn the attention from myself. I could feel people looking at me, probably judging me already.

But then I saw who was in the seat next to the empty ones.

Ellicia.

"We're leaving."

"What? Kyle? Hey, Kyle!"

I started to turn around and walk away when I felt Damon's hand grab my arm, pull me back. It drew a few dodgy glances from some of the spectators around us. A steward narrowed his eyes, paid close attention. Just what I needed. Another way to humiliate myself right in front of Ellicia.

"What you think you're doing?" Damon asked.

"Ellicia's there."

"And?"

"And? I can't be next to Ellicia. Not after the last few days. I just want... however the hell many minutes away from the school types. Not this."

"But man, I thought you'd like—"

"I'm catching the subway home," I said, as much as the thought of doing that alone terrified me. "I'll see you at... Wait. You thought I'd like what?"

Damon lowered his head. He cleared his throat. "I found out Ellicia was going. Heard a few of her friends talking about it."

I felt anger tingling inside. "You—"

"Hear me out, man. I'm just... I just thought it'd be good for you. Spend some time with the girl of your dreams."

I laughed. "The girl of my dreams? Dreams is the key word there, Damon. I don't stand a chance with her. Not one chance."

"She thinks you're cool, man," Damon said. "Just give her a chance."

"Me give her a chance? You're not getting what I'm saying. She thinks I'm hilarious."

"That's not a bad thing."

"No, I mean the bad kind of hilarious."

"And how the hell did you come to that conclusion?"

"She laughed at me in geography."

"Oh," Damon said. He scratched his head. "Yeah, that is kind of decisive. Sorry. Feel free to leave."

I couldn't believe right then that my own best friend had done this to me. He knew how much of a wuss I was when it came to girls—and when it came to anything, for that matter. I wasn't sure I'd be able to trust him again.

But then again, I knew he only had my best intentions at heart. As much of a daft move as it was, he gave a damn about my best interests, and this only went to show it.

"Damon, I'm sorry. I appreciate this. Really. But I can't be here."

Damon shook his head. "You're gonna be like this your whole life if you aren't careful."

I let out a sigh. "And that's my problem to deal with—"

"Kyle?"

The voice wasn't Damon's. It wasn't anybody's nearby.

In fact, it wasn't even a male voice.

It was a female.

Ellicia.

Damon stepped aside. Ellicia was leaning across the empty

seats. Her dark hair glistened in the spark of the floodlights. Her smile lit me up inside.

"Wow. It actually is you!"

I felt my face redden. I scratched the back of my neck, which tickled. I could feel myself getting warm. "Yeah. Hi." It was about as much as I could manage.

We stood there for a few seconds. Ellicia frowned. I didn't know what to do. Didn't know where to go.

The most remarkable thing about all this?

Ellicia was acting... nice.

"Well, are you sitting or are you standing?"

"Oh," I said. I looked at Damon, who raised his eyebrows, then back towards Ellicia. "Well, didn't want to take my chances. Thought I'd better stay close to the restrooms."

I knew the joke—or *attempt* at a joke—was awful and awkward and all kinds of self-deprecating horrible right away.

But something else strange happened.

Ellicia started to laugh.

I felt myself easing as she laughed. As she actually genuinely laughed at my joke. And I started to wonder if maybe sitting next to her and watching the game wasn't such a bad idea after all.

So I did it. I swallowed my nerves, fought every urge inside telling me to run away far away from here, and I walked down the row and sat beside Ellicia.

I wasn't sure I'd ever been this close to her. Funny when you're close to someone. You notice things you didn't even know existed when you were far away. A little gap between the teeth. A little freckle under the eye. The smell of sweet perfume.

Hell, more than anything, I noticed just how much more beautiful Ellicia actually was than I'd realized.

I didn't think that was possible. But it was.

And I was sat next to her.

And she was smiling at me.

This was not a dream.

I didn't say anything for a while. I listened to the loudspeaker announce the teams and stood up to clap. That's when Ellicia leaned over.

"Never knew you were into soccer," she said.

Shit. Shit. What was the cool thing to say?

"Yeah," I said. "Pretty big fan."

"Oh yeah? Who's your favorite player?"

Shitting shit.

I scanned my limited sports knowledge for the name of any random player.

"Um, Andy Murray, probably."

Ellicia burst out laughing. Her friend, who I recognized as Sally from school, did too.

"What?" I asked, feeling totally uneasy about what I'd just said. "You... you not like him?"

"Oh, I like Andy Murray," Ellicia said. "Just I didn't know he was such a big soccer player, being one of the best tennis players in the world, of course."

If a hole opened up in the earth right now, I'd happily plunge myself right into it.

"It's okay," Ellicia said, nudging my arm. "Everybody's gotta start somewhere."

It took me a little longer to realize what'd just occurred. Not only had I just made a complete and utter fool of myself in front of Ellicia; she'd let me off the hook. Again.

Nothing of the like had ever happened to me before.

I genuinely didn't know what to do, what to say, what to *think*.

Something else weird happened. We small talked. We chatted. Ellicia asked what my plans were for the summer. She asked me about my plans when I finally graduated from high school, and when I told her I was planning on taking a few months in paid work experience at a local law firm before moving on to college, I was relieved to hear she was staying local too, her heart set on Columbia.

And then the weirdest weird of all happened.

"Are you going to the party, then?"

Funnily enough, I hadn't really thought much about the end of year party. I'd never been to a single one, and I'd never had any plans to go. I mean, why would I go? I was a loser. I wasn't likely to be going with anyone. And I'd be even funnier and even more notable by my lack of a companion.

I dreamed of going to the party with Ellicia. But that wasn't happening.

And now here she was, asking me about the party.

I wanted to say yes. I wanted to tell her that I was going and that she was coming with me. I wanted to hold her in my arms while the crowd cheered and press my lips against hers.

But of course, what did I do?

"Nah. I'm not going."

I felt Damon smack me in the ribs and tried to keep my cool.

Ellicia lowered her head, turned her gorgeous blue eyes away from mine. "Oh. Oh, well... well, that's a shame."

Idiot. She's disappointed. She's actually disappointed.

I couldn't end it like this. I could tell her the truth.

She was disappointed I wasn't going to the party.

The girl of my dreams was disappointed I wasn't going to the party, and I was letting her be disappointed.

"Actually—"

The crowd lifted from their seats. I took an elbow to the chin, from Ellicia, which made my head spin.

Ellicia laughed as the crowd, Damon included, roared around me, celebrating a goal. She grabbed my arm. Pulled me up. Smiled and laughed. "Sorry," she said, grinning after the knock to the mouth.

I found myself looking back at her as she kept her hand on my arm.

I found myself looking into her eyes and smiling.

I wanted to tell her. I wanted to tell her right then that I was going to the party. Because I could feel it. I could feel the warmth in my chest. I could feel that sensation that they always tell you about in movies. The sensation where you just *know* someone is interested.

I couldn't believe it. I didn't think I'd ever been as happy as I was at this moment right now.

And then I heard a few blasts, a few screams, and saw a man with a rifle firing into the crowd.

Just meters away.

8

I looked into the eyes of the gunman and tried not to real-shit myself right there and then.

People threw themselves past me, hurtled away from the sounds of the blasts. The screams were getting louder inside the stadium as word of the attack spread like wildfire. On the field, I noticed the players had stopped playing, and were running away too.

Everyone was trapped. Trapped under the grips of the attack.

A gunman attack, right here at the soccer game I just so happened to be at.

I felt arms punch into me. Heard the screams getting louder. The gunman, who had a weird plastic black mask over his face, didn't seem to be targeting anyone in particular—just pointing his gun at whoever he could, shooting them down. I could smell the smoke from the gun, feel the heat from the bullets. My throat was filled with the taste of vomit.

I wanted to do something. More than anything, I wanted to help. No doubt everyone in this stadium wanted to help.

But I knew that I wanted something more than to help.

I wanted to disappear.

To get the hell out of this place.

"Kyle, quick!"

I heard Damon's voice. It was muffled, mixed in with all the shouts and screams. I turned around, saw him and Ellicia were now the other side of me. They were making their way down the row towards the exit. But so many people were trying to get through that exit that it looked compressed as though they were being crushed into a can like sardines.

"Come on!" Damon shouted.

I couldn't move. My knees were locked. I felt myself shaking all over. The memories came flying back. Memories of my past. Memories of the day of The Great Blast. The sound of the explosion ripping across Staten Island. Then the sounds of the screams—the screams of those who'd lost, the screams of my mom and dad as they found my sister.

I looked back over my shoulder.

The gunman was looking right into my eyes. Rifle raised.

I wanted to stay put. I wanted to disappear into a hole in the ground.

But I couldn't.

I had to run.

I ran as quickly as I could down the row and after Damon, Ellicia and her friends. I heard the gun fire another few times, but I didn't feel anything smack into my back so figured the gunman must've shot at someone else.

I got to the end of the row. Reached the mass of people trying to squeeze their way into the gate and get out of this place. It was chaos in the middle of these people. I could hear crying. The mass of people was so thick, everyone crushing against each other. I tried to take a deep breath but couldn't; I was stuck with the crowd, being dragged down those steps and into the turnstiles. I tried to move, but again, I couldn't. We were flowing. Flowing, like water.

Flowing, unable to breathe.

Head spinning.

Chest tightening...

I heard more gunshots behind us. Heard screams right beside me. I tasted something in the air. Something rusty. Like blood.

And I knew it was blood. I knew right away that it had to be blood. But I didn't want to accept it. I didn't want to accept that this gunman, for whatever reason, was firing at people inside a soccer stadium.

As I was dragged further down the steps and into turnstiles, towards the exit gate, I felt tears start to roll down my cheeks. If I'd just stayed at home, then this wouldn't have happened. If Damon hadn't booked for us to go to a stupid soccer match— something we *never* did—then we wouldn't be here. We wouldn't be caught up in this.

I thought about calling Mom. Telling her I loved her. But I wasn't strong enough to do that. I'd call her and blabber on at her to get down here and help me, which wasn't fair on her to hear.

No. I was alone. Alone, even though Damon and Ellicia were just a few people in front of me. They felt so far away.

I saw them battling their way down the stairs. The crowd of people thinned as they hurtled out of the exit gates. Damon and Ellicia reached it. They turned around, horror in their eyes. "Hurry up, Kyle!" Damon shouted.

I could see that he wanted to wait. That he wanted to try and help me get out.

But I knew that he couldn't.

It wasn't safe for him to stay.

"Please, man," he said. I could see redness in his eyes. "Please... just hurry."

"I'm coming," I said.

It was already too late.

Damon and Ellicia were out of the stadium.

I thought I'd felt alone earlier, but it was nothing on the feeling I felt now. A coldness covered me. I felt disconnected, completely disconnected from anyone or anything that could help me. And it scared me. It terrified me. I just wanted to get out of here—just wanted to get out of here and get back home and never step foot outside again. Never.

I battled my way through more of the people, desperate to take a deep breath. I could see the door getting closer. Hopefully, Damon and Ellicia would be outside, waiting for me. I'd be able to hold Ellicia's hand, hug her, tell her everything was going to be okay.

Because we'd been through this together. We had that in common. We'd both suffered here.

I reached the bottom step when somebody walked around the side of the turnstiles.

He was a dark haired man. He had a black mask pulled over his face, just like the gunman on the stands.

Everyone on the stairs froze.

It took a few seconds for anyone to realize what was happening.

A few seconds, as the man pulled a rifle from behind his back and started firing at the crowd.

I spun around. Went to run back up the stairs, heart racing, feeling myself scream. But somebody pushed me down. And then I could feel feet smacking into my back, knocking the air out of my lungs, stamping down on my ribs. I felt something crack, and it knocked the wind out of me.

More feet clambered down whenever I tried to rise to my

feet. I thought right then, the taste of blood strong in my mouth, that this was it. This was how I died. Crushed in a soccer stadium. Nothing more than a body on the floor.

And then I found the strength from somewhere inside me to stand.

To push my way up back into the crowd, gunfire sounding from both directions.

To hurtle past people, pushing my way through them, back up the stairs.

I wasn't sure where to go as I ran up the stairs. Wasn't sure whether to try turning around or go back out into the stadium, where most people would be gone; try getting down on the field.

But as I looked in front of me at the easiest possible destination, a bitter irony covered me. In all this chaos, in all this trauma, it actually made me laugh.

The restroom.

Of course I was running to the frigging restroom. Again.

I ran around the side of the restroom entrance. Threw myself past the sinks. There were more people inside. All of them battling for a cubicle to hide in, for somewhere to disappear until the attack was over.

I rushed for a door on my right, but it slammed and locked before I could get inside. I tried another, but that was locked too.

Behind, I heard shouting. More gunshots.

Shit. I had to be quick.

I reached the last two cubicles, the hope in my body disappearing. I tried the one next to the end... but shit, that was locked too.

I was about to give up when I felt the final door on my right drift open.

I looked inside it. Looked in at the white toilet, the tiny little area where I was confining myself to. Where there was no escape from.

More gunshots nearby.

I did the only thing I could.

I ran inside the toilet and slammed the door shut.

I fell back against the toilet. Sat there, gasping, sweating, heart racing. My teeth chattered. All I could see in my mind's eye were those gunmen firing at people. All I could hear echoing around my skull were those gunshots.

I tried to tell myself it was over. That everything was over. I thought about Cassie and begged her to make everything okay, to watch over me and make everything okay.

I tried.

But then I heard the footsteps strolling slowly into the restroom.

There was silence for a few seconds. A couple of worried gasps from the people in the cubicles beside me.

And then the person spoke.

"Come on, little piggies. The big bad wolf is here."

A cubicle door smashed open.

Gunfire rattled inside it.

They were coming. They were coming and there was nothing I could do.

9

Time stood still as I stood in that restroom cubicle and listened to the gunman's footsteps get closer.

I squeezed my eyes shut. I didn't want to see the cubicle around me. Like by not opening my eyes, there was less of a chance that I was actually here, somehow. That I might just wake up back home and realize this was all just one big messed-up nightmare.

But I heard another cubicle door smash open. I heard more gunshots.

And that sound, which made every inch of my body jump, reminded me that this wasn't a dream.

This was reality.

Cold, hard reality.

I tasted sick on my tongue. I wanted to throw up, the smell of the gunfire triggering my gag reflex. But through everything, it was that memory of Cassie dying in front of me when I was just eight that came to my mind. That memory of The Great Blast—the moment my life, my family's life, changed forever.

I felt tears roll down my cheeks, felt my body shake, and I prayed that Cassie could help somehow.

Another door kicked in.

More gunshots.

How wonderfully ironic. Just days ago, I'd been mocked in front of the whole school for running to the restroom to get out of a football game. Now here I was, trapped in a toilet cubicle once again.

Only this time, Ellicia wasn't the one coming to the door. Mr. Preacher from history wasn't the one coming to the door.

The person coming to the door was going to kill me.

I thought back to the time of the ULTRAs as the footsteps got nearer. I wondered if anything like this would be allowed to happen when Orion was around. He stopped loads of incidents like this. Terrorism ended the day Orion and the rest of the Heroes—the pre-ULTRA days—soared above the earth.

But since the end of the ULTRAs, the world was getting back to how it used to be again.

This time, nobody was coming to help me.

I felt every muscle in my body tense as the footsteps stopped right outside my door. I wanted to disappear. I wanted to be invisible. I wanted to go away and—

A bang.

A bang, to my right.

The cubicle to my right flew open.

They'd walked past me. They'd walked right past my cubicle.

"Wrap it up, Scott," a voice said. "We're done here."

I couldn't believe it as I listened to the men disappear. They'd walked away from my cubicle. One moment, I'd been sitting there, eyes closed, waiting.

I'd felt a tingling sensation spread up the back of my neck.

And then I'd heard a sound to my right. The sound of a cubicle door being kicked in.

I stayed still. Stayed completely still for a few seconds.

When I opened my eyes, I couldn't believe what I was looking at.

The cubicle door in front of me was open. Wide open. It made my skin shiver.

I hadn't heard them kick my cubicle door down. And if they had, why hadn't they shot me?

Something wasn't right. Something just didn't feel right at all.

And then something else weird struck me, as the sound of the footsteps disappeared further from the restroom.

I'd heard a cubicle on the right being kicked in. Only that was weird because there was no cubicle on the right. I'd been in the last cubicle. I was sure of it.

I didn't want to walk towards the cubicle door. I wanted to close it and wait in here until someone came in and saved me. The cubicle thing got to me, creeped me out. Maybe I'd just got caught up in the moment. Maybe I hadn't run into the last cubicle after all. My attention was understandably elsewhere when the gunmen had chased me into the restroom.

That's all it was. Confusion. My mind playing tricks on me.

I didn't even consider that the glass smashing in my classroom and this had anything to do with each other. Not just yet.

I held my breath. I could hear silence outside. Silence, and a few groans from fallen people. I didn't want to move. I was shaking so hard that I wasn't sure I *could* move.

But Damon. Ellicia. My parents. They'd be worried about me. They'd be so worried. I had to get out of this place—to take any chance I had to get away.

I took a few deep breaths—breaths I knew damned well might be my last. And then I walked closer towards the open cubicle door.

Walking wasn't easy. My legs felt like jelly. Every step I

made, I was convinced my feet were going to just collapse underneath me, that my knees were just going to give way.

But they couldn't. They couldn't because I had to get out of here. I had to get out of this stadium and had to get home.

And I could never step foot near this place again. Ever.

I reached the cubicle door. My heartbeat pulsated up my neck. I peeked around the side of the cubicle door. Looked for any sign of movement, any sign of life.

The mirrors in the restroom were smashed. So too were some of the sinks. On the floor, bullets.

I tried not to look at the blood.

I wiped my forehead and then gritted my teeth together to stop them chattering. I thought about just stepping back. Going back inside that cubicle and hiding in there. I'd got lucky. Somehow, I'd...

When I turned around to the right, something sent a shiver up my spine.

I wasn't in the cubicle at the end. I'd realized that much earlier.

But I wasn't even in the cubicle *next* to the end.

I was right on the other side of the cubicles. Nine, ten cubicles, all to my right.

I stared down at them, unable to get my head around what'd happened, unable to understand how I'd got where I was, when I heard footsteps approaching the restroom.

I stepped back. Closed my eyes again. Stayed as still as I possibly could.

"You hear something?" a voice asked.

Silence. Then, "Thought I did. Never mind. Let's get down to the field and get the hell outta here."

I listened to the footsteps run away again. I opened my eyes. I was convinced the speaker had been right in front of the open door of this cubicle. But then, they can't have been. They'd have seen me.

"Let's get down to the field and get the hell outta here..."

Those words echoed in my mind. I knew I had my opportunity to escape, my chance to flee. They were going down to the field, so I had to find my way down the steps and towards the door. I couldn't stick around here. I couldn't risk it, not anymore. I'd taken my chances as it was.

I took a deep breath—similarly difficult as the last few I'd taken—and then walked towards the cubicle door.

I didn't look to my side. If I had, I'd have realized right there and then that something seriously weird was happening.

I was in a different cubicle again.

I just didn't know it yet.

I walked past the broken glass, past the fragments of sink and mirror all over the floor. I kept my eyes ahead. I didn't want to look around. Didn't want to see the chaos the gunmen had caused.

I just had to keep moving.

I just had to get out.

I stepped towards the exit of the restroom. Looked to the left. Clear. Then to the right. Totally clear.

"Please," I mumbled, my lips quivering. "Please."

And then I walked as quickly as I could over to those stairs.

When I reached them, adrenaline spinning through my body, I was pleasantly surprised to see the door at the bottom of the stairs open. The exit. Nobody was guarding it. My way out was right ahead.

I went to take a step when I felt something behind me.

Felt... like I was being watched.

I turned around, and every muscle in my body gave in.

One of the gunmen stood opposite. He was looking right into my eyes. Smiling.

His gun was pointed right at my chest.
"Sweet dreams, kid."
I squeezed my eyes shut and held my breath.
The gunman pulled the trigger.

10

I felt the darkness surrounding me as the gunshot rattled through the air.

I waited. Waited for the bullet to hit me. I could hear the gunshot firing at me as if in slow motion. Tears streamed down my cheeks, their saltiness hitting my lips. My body froze all over. In my mind's eye, I saw Cassie; I saw her lying there in the road as the explosion of The Great Blast surrounded me.

And then I saw Ellicia. The way she'd smiled at me. The way she hadn't judged me. Despite everything that'd happened.

I saw her, and in that millisecond since hearing the gun fire and the bullet hitting me, I wished I'd had more guts. More guts to tell her how I felt. More guts to stand up for myself. To be as strong as I knew I could be. Because I was strong. I was strong because I'd had to be with the upbringing I'd experienced. I had to be after losing my older sister.

I waited for the bullet to pierce my skin and for the darkness to get a whole lot darker.

I realized then that I'd been waiting a long time. A hell of a long time.

I didn't want to open my eyes. I didn't want to see what was in front of me.

But I had to.

I opened my eyes.

I didn't understand what I was looking at at first. It just didn't make sense. Didn't add up, in my mind.

The gunman who'd pointed the gun at my chest pulled the trigger, was lying on the floor.

There was a bullet hole right in the middle of his head.

I looked down at him. Still frozen. Part of me wondered whether this was some kind of trick. Whether it was a plot to scare me, to toy with me.

But there was no denying the reality of the gunshot wound on the gunman's forehead.

I walked over to him, slowly, shaking. I wanted to pick up the gun. I could use it to defend myself if I needed to. But then that was a stupid idea. The police would think I was one of them. They'd shoot me down before I had a chance to even explain myself.

The police. They must've been here. They must've got in here and shot the gunman down before he had a chance to...

No. I'd heard the gunman pull the trigger. And I'd only heard that one bullet. I'd *seen* his fingers tighten around the trigger.

The bullet he'd fired should be inside me.

I should be dead. Or at least, wounded.

But I wasn't. I was standing. I was alive.

I stepped back. Started to head towards the steps. A weird feeling took over my body. Thoughts about that cubicle, how it felt like I'd shifted between them when I needed to most. And then the incident back at school. The windows smashing when I was at my angriest. When I felt that sadness and frustration in the form of a weird tingling sensation, just like I had one other time in my life more than any.

The day of The Great Blast.

I started to descend the steps. What was I thinking? That something happened on the day of The Great Blast to make me... well, to make me what? No. I was being stupid. I was in shock. It was natural.

I had a guardian angel looking out for me. That's all it was. Luck was on my side, for the first time in my stupid life.

I got halfway down the steps when I saw someone appear through the door in front of me.

It didn't take me long to realize it was another one of the gunmen.

He lifted his gun. Went to fire.

I felt the anger, the fear, just like I'd felt it before.

I felt the tingling sensation take over my body.

I jumped. Jumped to the right as the bullet fired from the gunman's gun.

I jumped over onto the wall. Ran down the side of it, not really in control of myself, not knowing what I was doing, just that the gunman was firing at me, and I had to stop him.

I jumped off the wall to the right and spun in midair as the gunman looked on, open mouthed. And then I landed right behind him. Pulled back my right fist and punched him. Hard.

He went flying.

Not backward, but upward.

Up onto the top level that I'd just run down from.

And...

Shit. I was back up there with him.

I felt the gunman reach for his gun, which was by his side. I looked at it, my body fully taken over by that tingling sensation, and the gun just flew out of his grip, then snapped in midair.

I looked down at the gunman and saw him start to lurch. Start to struggle to find his words.

I lifted him up. Threw him back against the wall. He stayed there. Stuck there, as I directed that fear, that anger, towards him.

As I looked up at him, the reality of my situation dawned on me. The reality of what was happening. Of why the weird things had been happening to me these entire few days.

I dropped the gunman back to the floor. Tied his hands behind his back, twisting them around one another in a bone-snapping knot.

And I did all of this with my mind. Nothing else.

I looked on, heart racing, feeling stronger than I'd ever felt before. I didn't understand what was happening to me. I didn't understand how I'd just done what I'd done, why I'd been able to do what I'd just done.

But as the gunman struggled and writhed around, hands knotted behind his back, I knew one thing for certain.

The windows in class smashing.

The movement between cubicles.

The... strength. That was all I could call it. The strength I'd shown to defeat these gunmen.

These weren't the abilities of a normal person. These weren't things normal, everyday humans were supposed to be able to do.

These were the abilities of ULTRAs.

So why the hell did I have them?

The thought of having ULTRA abilities punched me in the stomach with its dark realization. ULTRAs were the enemy. They were hated by the masses for the destruction they'd caused, particularly in New York and The Great Blast, as well as the great three-year battle between Orion and Saint. Sure, they'd done good things when they were Heroes. But their intentions, their morals, were always under the microscope.

Besides, ULTRAs didn't exist anymore. The ULTRAs were gone. The era was a dark footnote in history.

But I had the abilities of an ULTRA.

I thought back to that day. The day of the Great Blast. I always wondered why I hadn't died. My sister died. Other people in the streets died. And sure, there were many random survivors. But I hadn't even had a scratch on me.

I'd felt something inside me that day. The same tingling feeling that had been emerging within these last few days whenever I was upset, angry, mad.

I'd felt it, and I started to understand.

There had to be a link.

Something happened on the day of The Great Blast.

Something terrifying happened to me, and it was only just starting to wake up, eight years later.

I walked away from the gunman. Backed off as the sound of sirens filled the outside.

My head spun with the adrenaline. I felt sick with the revelation.

I was an ULTRA.

I was an ULTRA, and there was nothing I could—

I saw the movement in the corner of my eye.

Saw the masked person—another gunman—raise the butt of their gun.

And before I could think to react, they smacked me in the side of my head, and everything went black.

11

I felt the sickness in my stomach. I felt something in my lungs. Heaviness, like I was surrounded by water.

I could hear voices echoing above me. Someone trying to push me down. I wanted to cry because it's all I could do, all I was capable of.

I saw that I was small. Smaller than I'd thought. Not as strong as I wanted to be. Not as strong as I needed to be.

"He'll be okay," a muffled voice said. "He always is."

I knew the voice. I recognized it from somewhere. I...

Then, I saw the light above, and I snapped out of my dreams.

I was lying down. Lying down somewhere. I wasn't sure where I was, only that it was so bright above me. I could hear beeping from somewhere to my left. I was vaguely aware of a figure standing by my side, saying things to me, but it was all so muffled and distorted that I couldn't make sense of it, not really.

I thought I must be back at home. Back in my bed. But then this couldn't be my home, this couldn't be my bed because there was never a light that bright above it.

"Kyle? You okay, son? You okay?"

I heard the voice and recognized it. Mom. I was pleased to hear her voice for some reason. Relieved. I wasn't sure why, or what, but it felt like I'd been through something. Like something had happened to me. Something big. Something...

I tasted vomit and blood in my mouth.

My body tensed.

The soccer stadium. I'd been at the soccer stadium with Damon. We'd seen Ellicia there and... shit, me and Ellicia had been talking to each other. We'd been getting on fine.

And then...

I remembered the sounds of the gunshots and it made me think back to the explosion again. The Great Blast.

I'd run. I'd run away from the gunmen. Damon and Ellicia got out. Or at least I hoped they got out. And as I'd been running, another gunman appeared at the exit gate, and I'd gone back inside, gone to the restroom.

"Oh, you're awake," Mom said. I could hear the shakiness in her voice. She leaned over. Stroked my head. Kissed it. "Thank the Lord you're awake."

I widened my eyes, as sore and tired as they were.

I saw then that I was in a hospital bed. Blue curtains were wrapped around my bed. I could hear coughs and beeping from others in the ward, but I was cocooned in my own little zone here. The back of my head hurt like mad.

"How you feeling?" Mom asked. Her eyes were dark underneath. Her face was pale. She didn't look like she'd been sleeping well lately.

I pushed myself up, but doing so made me ache some more.

"Oh, you keep still," Mom said. She eased me back down onto the bed, adjusted my pillow. "Don't move if you don't have to. Don't want you hurting yourself."

"What—what happened?"

Mom backed away. She held on to my hand. Looked into my eyes with wide-eyed severity. "You really don't remember?"

I pushed myself to try and remember what she might be talking about. The attacks, yes. But what else? There was something else.

I'd run into the restroom and...

My skin went cold.

I remembered.

I was locked in that cubicle. Waiting for the gunman to reach my location. Only he hadn't arrived. Well, he had. But for some reason, somehow, I'd shifted to another cubicle.

I'd closed my eyes, embraced the fear inside me, and I'd shifted to another cubicle.

My heart pounded. My hands shook a little.

"You okay, Kyle? Your dad's on his way soon, Son. He's been here by your side all this time. Just gone to grab himself a coffee."

I swallowed the phlegmy lump in my throat. The memories kept on rolling back through my consciousness. I'd left that restroom. I'd reached the stairs. But then a gunman had pointed his gun at me, shot at me.

Only when I opened my eyes, he was lying dead on the floor.

I was still standing.

"I told him to cut down on coffee," Mom said. "Read online that it's bad for the nerves."

Then there was the other incident. The main incident. The one that hit me even harder than anything else so far.

I'd attacked one of the gunmen. I'd run along the side of a vertical wall, jumped acrobatically down onto him, and taken him out. And then I'd lifted him up with a strength that went far beyond my own abilities. Tied his hands behind his back in an impossible knot.

I'd done things no human should be able to do.

I'd done things only an ULTRA was supposed to be able to do.

"You've gone pale," Mom said. "You sure you're okay?"

I cleared my throat. Made a conscious effort to give Mom some of my attention. "Yeah," I said. "Just... sore head."

"Of course it's sore," Mom said. "It's amazing you ain't sore anywhere else. Doctors thought you were gonna be unconscious for days. That you took a nasty knock to the head, but... but somehow you're all okay. All the scans, everything's okay."

There was a pause. I considered my mom's words. Was that something to do with the powers I had? It had to be. Scared me, but it had to be true.

So I could heal myself, too. I really was... well. Not just any old ULTRA. A special kind of ULTRA.

Great.

"Do you still not remember what happened in that place?"

I wasn't sure how in detail to go when speaking to Mom. I'd realized what I could do. Perhaps I could dismiss it as adrenaline, but no. The things I'd done, they were ULTRA abilities. Unmistakable ULTRA abilities. And damned strong ones, too. Speed. What seemed like teleportation. Strength. Telekinesis. Dammit, I didn't just have one ability. I had a whole truckload of 'em.

But I couldn't tell Mom that. I couldn't tell anyone that. Because being an ULTRA was more dangerous than being one of those gunmen who shot up the soccer stadium.

And being an ULTRA with as many powers as I had...

"Damon," I said. "And..."

"Damon's fine," Mom said. "So too's your other friend. That girl. Elle, or something?"

"Ellicia," I said.

Mom nodded. "Both fine. Both got out okay."

"How long have I..."

"Just the night," Mom said. "Gave us a scare, though, Kyle. Doctors said you were out cold like I said. But then you started showing serious levels of brain activity, or something. Like you were conscious all along. And then everything just... fixed itself. Like nothin' they've ever seen."

I knew I'd have to be careful if I didn't want my ULTRA abilities exposing already. "Right," I said. "Weird."

"Kyle, I... I don't know how much you rem—"

"I remember a lot of shooting. I remember running away. Then... then I remember getting stamped on. And not much after that."

Mom nodded like she was trying to conjure up a mental picture of what I was saying. "My boy," she said. I saw her lips quivering. "My sweet boy."

She hugged me. And I felt tears building at my eyelids as she held on. I'd come close to dying in that stadium. Any normal human being and I'd be dead. But something saved me.

No. *I* saved me.

I was an ULTRA.

For better or for worse, I was an ULTRA.

I had to learn to deal with that one way or other.

"The police. They want to speak to you. About some... some CCTV footage or something."

My stomach dropped. Shit. CCTV. Of course. They'd have footage of me doing... well, whatever I was doing. They'd figure out I was an ULTRA right away. I couldn't let them speak to me. Couldn't let them get to me. It wasn't safe.

"I'm... I'm really tired," I lied.

"I know, sweetie," Mom said, turning her head to one side, stroking my fringe some more. "And this'll all be over soon and you can come back home. But they said it's really important they check something with you. Let me know when it's okay for me to call them in."

Call them in?

I became aware of voices outside the curtain. Of footsteps walking backward and forward across the hard hospital floor. Dammit. They were outside already. They were outside, and they were going to take me away. Or worse—they were going to kill me.

I felt that tingling sensation growing inside me but it felt weaker than before, less focused. Maybe they were using something. If they suspected I was an ULTRA, they must have a way to repress my powers.

I was finished. This was over.

"I'll call them in—"

"Mom, wait!"

But it was already too late.

The curtains opened up. Outside the curtain, I saw two police officers standing there. Both of them were dressed in black suits, wearing sunglasses like they were from the Men in Black or something.

Both of them had little yellow FBI logos on their jackets.

"Kyle Peters," the officer on the left said, a bald black guy with a deep voice. "Detective Agent Kirsh. And this is Detective Agent Cole."

The man beside Kirsh nodded. He had a broad head and a big figure that I didn't want to mess with anytime soon.

I thought about using what I'd discovered to teleport my way out of this. But it was just too dangerous. Too risky. Besides, I wasn't even sure I *could* replicate those abilities.

"Obviously, we're sorry to intervene right now. You must be traumatized. But we have to ask you a few questions."

Here it comes...

"The CCTV we retrieved was down. Completely fried."

Wait. What?

"So we aren't able to gather any footage of what happened inside the stands. The gunmen must've shot down the cameras some way, I don't know."

Cole interrupted: "But we believe some of the gunmen got away. And strangely, it looks like some kind of fight went on in there before we got there. Some kind of in-fighting between them. Broken bones. Bullets fired. Seeing as we found you in there, we were wondering if you saw anything?"

I looked between Kirsh and Cole. My heart still pounded. I couldn't believe my luck at the CCTV being taken out. They didn't know. They genuinely didn't know.

Or, they were testing me.

I wanted to tell them the truth. That several of the gunmen had got away. That *I'd* been the one to stop the ones who didn't.

But instead, I said the only things I could, the only things I knew would keep me safe. For now.

"I remember running," I said. "Then I remember... I remember being knocked down and stamped on. I remember passing out. Then I remember waking up."

Silence between me and the two officers.

"So you don't remember how many of these gunmen there might've been? Where they might've gone to?"

I searched my mind and played my words carefully. "No. Well, maybe something about going out onto the field to get away. But I don't know. It's hard to say. I don't remember a..."

I started coughing. This brought our conversation to an end.

The officers sighed and walked towards the curtain. "You're a very lucky man, Mr. Peters. Eighty-nine people died in that stadium. You're fortunate to have a guardian angel looking over you. Rest well."

They disappeared, but before they did, I swore I caught a look of suspicion in their eyes.

I did have a guardian angel looking over me.

His name was Kyle Peters.

And if I wasn't careful, Kyle Peters was going to get me in big trouble.

12

Three days home from hospital confined to my bedroom and remarkably, I was eager to get out.

I hobbled down the stairs. I could smell chicken curry fumes sneaking up from the kitchen. It smelled good, even though I hadn't been hungry since I woke up. I'd been out cold for a day. The doctor told me and my parents that it'd take time for me to get my appetite back.

But deep down, I knew the real reason why I wasn't eating well.

I walked towards my front door. I didn't want to get into a deep conversation with Mom about where I was going. She'd only worry.

I hoped to sneak out as the chicken sizzled in the pan. As the fumes from the spices made me cough.

"Where you off to?"

Dad's voice made my stomach sink. I turned around. Looked back at him. "Just out."

Dad's eyes narrowed. That pallid look that had covered his face for the last eight years was there as strong as ever. "You sure that's a good idea, Son?"

I scratched the back of my neck. "Yeah. I mean, I can't stay cooped up in that bedroom forever."

"Where you off to, then?"

"Just... just Damon's."

"Damon's?"

I nodded, feeling my cheeks flushing. I'd never been good at lying to my dad. But I couldn't tell him the truth. How could I possibly begin to tell him the truth?

"Don't be long. Dinner'll be ready in an hour, tops."

"I'm just checking in on him, that's all. I'll be back in no time."

I smiled at Dad. And for a moment, I thought that smile might just look convincing.

Dad nodded. "Good." He turned around.

I lowered the handle and went to step outside.

"Stay safe, Son."

Dad's words made my chest well down. "I will, Dad."

I walked out into the cool summer air, the sounds of the city a distant murmur.

I wasn't going to Damon's. I'd checked in on Damon a few times, sure, and he was doing... well, he was doing okay after the attack. Not amazing. How could anyone be doing amazing? He was just okay.

But I had something else to do.

I was going to somewhere else entirely.

WHEN DAD WAS YOUNGER, before the Great Blast, he ran a pretty decent car mechanics shop over on the north side of Staten Island right by the ferry terminal. Peters' Parts, it was called. Decent business. Never made him rich, but enough for the family to get by in one of the most expensive cities in the world.

Soon after the Great Blast, after Carrie's death, Dad kind of let that place go to ruin. He tried selling it, but the building was in such a state after years of ill maintenance that he could never get rid of it. He sold everything worth something inside it, gutted it as well as he could, but he still technically owned that garage. Nowadays, he worked part-time at a grocery store just a few blocks away from our home. Mom worked reception at a salon in the day, and sometimes the late shift at a hotel bar at night. I figured she brought in most of the money. But she seemed alright about that. She seemed content.

I stood outside the chain linked fences surrounding it, the rain lashing down from the dark clouds above. I was a long way from Damon's. I was a long way from home.

But I was exactly where I needed to be.

I looked up at the chain linked fence. I knew I could try using my powers right away to get inside Peters' Parts, but I didn't want to draw any attention to myself.

I climbed over the chain linked fence, looking left and right, making sure no one was onto me. My hood was pulled over my head. I knew I probably looked like a criminal, but fortunately, most people around Staten Island knew there wasn't much worth stealing in Peters' Parts after all.

I dropped down the other side. Felt a stitch biting at my stomach. Already, I was out of breath. Damn. This was why I needed to think about exercising more. And no, Wii Sports did *not* count as exercise.

I ran across the gravel. One of the windows at the side of the garage was smashed and covered in cobwebs. Hopefully, I wouldn't have to use that window. I was pushing my luck as it was. Rather just walk in through the door. Rather just...

The door was locked.

Shit.

I stood beneath the smashed window and looked up at it. I

could jump up there and squeeze my way inside. I'd have to be careful I wasn't being watched—I'd already been let off the hook by the CCTV gods once as it was. And I didn't fancy explaining what I was doing here to Dad. Not one bit.

My skin crawled as I pictured the rats crawling around inside there. Or cutting my hands on infected glass. Ugh.

But I had to get inside. The harder it was to get inside this place, the better. Because it meant I wasn't going to be seen.

And with what I was planning, I couldn't be seen.

I jumped up. Gripped onto the side of the window ledge with my palms. I didn't have much upper body strength, but I used what little I did have to pull myself up, drag myself inside.

I felt loose shards of glass nicking at my bare skin, cutting at my hoodie. Inside the garage, total darkness. I could smell mustiness. Damp. And weirdly, weed and urine, like someone had been hanging out in here.

The thought of dropping into a hobo's den sent shivers up my spine.

But halfway through the window, I didn't really have much choice.

I landed hard on the solid floor. I stood up, dusted myself down, winded once again. I couldn't hear anything in here. Nothing but things scuttling about. I could feel cobwebs against my face and swore I felt little spiders creeping along my neck.

I searched. Searched for a light source.

And then I realized my stupidity.

Of course there wasn't gonna be a light source. Dad had left this place for dead. No way he was going to still be paying for...

Weird thing happened when I pressed down the light switch.

The lights flickered on.

They were dim. Not the full beam they used to be. But they were there.

I wondered if Mom knew Dad was still paying for electricity in this place. And I wondered *why* he was still paying for electricity in this place.

I looked around. The room was as I'd remembered as a little boy, only a sad fossil of what it used to be. There was the spine of an old red car in the middle of the room. An Escort, or something. Looked pretty cool, but it'd need a lot of work to get in order; work this place wasn't seeing any of. The floor was covered in dust and mud. Water dripped down from the roof above, covering the old car manuals, which were already so soaked they were going moldy.

It felt sad, seeing this place in such a condition. It used to be my dad's life. And just like my dad's life, it was nothing now.

But I didn't have time to feel sad.

I was here for a reason.

I wasn't sure how to feel about discovering I had ULTRA capabilities. Mostly terrified, which was consistent with my overall character, I figured. But I'd be damned if I didn't learn if I could recreate those powers. Or at least figure out *how* to use them.

I turned to a wooden beam sticking through the middle of the room. Held my breath. Pulled back my fist.

I cracked it into the wooden beam.

I yelped with the pain. The beam didn't even dint. Shit. I could've tried something lighter first. If anyone saw me, they'd think I was mad.

I held my breath and tried again. And then I tried jumping onto the wall just like I had in the stadium.

I ran towards it. Ran with as much confidence and power as I could.

I could do this. I could climb this wall and I could run along it. I'd done it before so I could do it again.

I could—

My feet hit the side of the wall.

I ran up it, just a little.

And then I went hurtling back to the floor, ass first.

I kept on trying, as much as I wanted to give up. I felt irritation growing inside me as I landed on my ass for the seventy-fifth time in the space of ten minutes. It was a quarter to eight, so I had to be back in fifteen minutes. What a waste of time I'd spent in here. I hadn't learned a thing, only that I was just as useless as I'd always been.

Part of me was relieved. Because I didn't want to be burdened with those abilities. I didn't want to be public enemy number one.

But part of me felt disappointed, too. Because when I'd used those powers, I didn't feel utterly useless. I felt strong.

Not like the kid who fake-shat himself in the toilet last week.

Not like...

When the embarrassment hit me, I saw a pencil drop off a flat work surface on the other side of the room, hit the floor.

I felt a tingling feeling in my stomach. And it reminded me of how I'd felt at the stadium two days ago. It reminded me of the fear I'd felt. The embarrassment I'd felt.

It reminded me of the pain I'd felt.

The pain of losing Cassie.

I let go of my breath.

Tensed my fist.

And then I walked over to the wooden beam and rammed my fist through it.

I couldn't believe what I was witnessing at first. I couldn't believe I'd actually done what I'd done.

But the middle of the beam came flying out.

My knuckles didn't even hurt.

I laughed. Felt a smile of amazement spreading across my

cheeks. My fear. My pain. My embarrassment. They were strong feelings. They were what made me feel strong. Brought out my powers.

I focused on that feeling, that tingling feeling, once again, and then I jumped across the room.

I went further than I thought was possible. And sure, I landed on my ass like an untrained gymnast, but the fact was I'd done it. I'd discovered my powers. I'd discovered that I did have the abilities of an ULTRA, whether I liked it or not.

I saw the Great Blast in my mind. Saw Orion and Saint fighting above me. I saw Cassie running towards me, telling me to go back.

I heard the Escort in front of me starting to creak. And as I focused on the pain of my mom and dad's screams as they lifted Cassie's body from the road, I felt a weight in my mind.

The car lifted further off the ground without me even touching it.

Further and further.

I saw Orion.

I saw Saint.

I saw all the chaos they'd caused.

And with the anger inside me, I tossed the car over to the other side of the garage.

I watched it move through the air as if in slow motion. Watched it power towards the wall of this place, ready to smash to pieces.

And then I saw movement outside the door of the garage.

I heard a key.

"Who's in there?"

My stomach dropped. I grabbed the car with my mind. Stopped it hitting the wall. Dad. Dad shouldn't be here. Why would he be here?

I didn't have time to think.

The door opened.
Dad stepped inside.
I held my breath.

13

Martin Peters looked around the garage and tried to figure out what the hell was going on.

It was rainy as hell outside. He'd come down here to check there weren't any more leaks. Always made sure he kept an eye on this place when it rained heavily. It wouldn't be the first time this place flooded. Besides, he wouldn't want his vintage red Ford Escort to get ruined.

He'd not been in this place for years until recently when he decided to work on an old Escort for Kyle. He figured it could be a decent birthday present for him. A cool, classic car, modeled to run perfectly in today's world. His son was a good kid, and he'd missed out on the last few years of his life. If he could provide him with that special something, especially after all the hell that'd been going on lately, he'd be happy. Happy he could put a smile on that boy's face again. A real smile.

He thought back to the times he used to spend in this place. Peters' Parts was never thriving, but it got busy. He missed the jokes and laughs between himself and his workmates. He missed the smell of petrol, first thing every morning. Looking back, he felt a kind of sadness as the truth struck him: he'd lived the best days of his life in this place. He'd peaked, and it'd been all downhill from there.

He stepped further inside the garage. Looked around. His heart pumped. He swore he'd seen someone in here when he was approaching. Swore he'd heard something. And the light was on, too. Someone had been here, whether he liked the thought or not.

But there were no signs of a break-in.

Everything was exactly in its place. Where it was meant to be.

Even the Escort.

He walked over to it. Put a hand on it. The surface of it was crazily clean. The rest of the room was dusty, but not that Escort.

Weird. He didn't know what to think of that. Didn't know what to make of it.

Not until he saw the smashed window at the side of the garage.

He tilted his head to one side and sighed. "Dammit," he muttered. "That's how they got in here."

He walked over to it. Took a close look. He was gonna have to get that fixed tomorrow. CCTV might catch the criminals, but it didn't stop 'em.

But for now, as Martin looked around, it didn't seem like anything was amiss in this place. Didn't seem like anything was off.

When he kept completely still, though, he got that weird sensation up the back of his neck. The kind you get when someone's watching you, only you don't know where they are.

He stood still. Tried to listen for sounds, catch any movement in the corner of his eyes.

He turned around and saw something standing right at the back of the room.

It had the shape of Kyle, his son. But what would his son be doing here? Why would Kyle be...

When Martin blinked, Kyle had gone.

He frowned. He swore he'd seen Kyle standing right there, looking back at him with that petrified look on his face he seemed to have most of the time.

He walked over to the spot, slowly. Kept his eyes on it. "Kyle?"

No sound in return. No movement. And nowhere Kyle could've hidden. No place at all.

He tutted. He musta been tired. That was it. He was just tired and seeing things. Wouldn't be the first time.

But still, he stood there a little while longer. Looked at that spot where he'd seen his son for a split second, as real as day. He waited to see if he showed himself again. If he emerged in his vision, just like he had before.

When he didn't, Martin walked over to the door, hit the lights and stepped out.

I LET GO of my deep breath and released my camouflage.

Adrenaline coursed through my system. Dad had looked right into my eyes, right *through* my eyes, and he hadn't said a word. He'd stood right up to my face and looked right through me.

My heart raced as the rain lashed down on the roof above. I heard every raindrop as if in slow motion. I saw everything in this room in complete order, which I'd managed to do in the space of a second.

I was everything I suspected.

I was everything I feared.

I was the last ULTRA.

14

I expected my return to school to be just as it was beforehand. Picking up where I'd left off. Going back into a world where I was the butt of the jokes.

Except it wasn't.

That was the greatest surprise of the many surprises this week.

I sat in the school yard against the wall with Damon. It was lunchtime, and the sun was out, which meant everyone was outside. Not that we ever sat our lunch inside. Not even in the thick of winter did we do that. We liked to pretend it was because we were cool, but in fact, it's just 'cause we weren't cool enough to sit in the main canteen. We'd draw far too much attention, simply because we were losers.

"Damn," Damon said. He sat beside me munching down on an apple. "I think I preferred it when people didn't treat us like we're ghosts."

"Speak for yourself," I said.

"It's weird, though, right? How... how what happened to us can just have changed how everyone is with us. Just like that." He clicked his finger.

I knew what Damon said was right. People walked through the school yard, glanced over at us. People that would usually stop to have their say, one way or other. But the bulk of them just ignored us today. Let us off the hook, like we'd been through enough as it was.

"Is it true what happened to you guys?" one of the younger kids asked.

Damon wiped his hands together. Stood up, half-smile on his face. "If you've heard the story about me scaring the gunmen away, then it's all true."

"I didn't hear that."

"Well, now you have."

The kids looked at Damon and me like we were strange for a few seconds, then off they ran.

"Why're people treating us like we're, like, kinda cool?" Damon asked.

I shrugged. "Probably something to do with us being at a soccer game in the first place. Which is cooler than anything we've ever done."

"I'll tell you what's cool," Damon said, dragging me to my feet. "Ellicia. She's cool."

My stomach turned. "Yeah. She is."

"You two were really hitting it off the other night, too."

"Yeah. Before gunmen ran into the stadium and started—"

"You were hitting it off. And you know you were. Man, have you even spoken to her since... since what happened?"

I felt guilt building inside. Truth was, I hadn't spoken to Ellicia since the attack at the stadium. I knew I probably should. She'd been through a traumatic event—all of us had. It was something that'd stay with us 'til the day we passed away.

But truth was, I'd had other things on my mind.

Like being an ULTRA.

"I mean, the party's coming up. And she did mention that,

didn't she?"

I shook my head and walked away. "The party's not an option."

Damon punched my arm. "Of course the party's an option, asshole. Especially now you've climbed the cool stakes."

"I didn't exactly do anything heroic in that stadium," I lied.

"No, maybe not—well, *obviously* not—you're Kyle Peters. But you've got the whole mystery vibe going on right now. The whole survivor vibe. You should use it, man. Use it before it goes stale. I know I am."

I stopped walking. "I don't know. I mean, I want to, but..."

"Then do it. Ask her to the party. Go on. See, she's over there now."

I turned around and saw Ellicia walking along with two of her friends, one of them Sally, who was at the game the other night. There were a few bruises on Ellicia's head. She was smiling, but I could tell it was the kind of smile that wasn't exactly beaming happiness.

"You did good the other day. We all did good. We did something tougher than any asshole in this school's had to do. So go up to her. Ask how the girl's doin', at least. Not heard of being gentlemanly?"

Damon burped before I had a chance to answer. "No. I guess I'll have to take lessons from you."

I didn't want to go over to Ellicia. Truth was, even though I had ULTRA abilities, I was still the same nervous little loser of a human underneath them.

But Damon was right. This was a chance to start a conversation with her. And I wouldn't get a better chance than this.

I tightened my fists and walked right over to her.

She saw me when I got close to her. Her blue eyes met mine, glistened in the sunlight. She smiled, and it was the most natural smile I'd seen on her face.

"Hey, Kyle," she said.

I scratched the back of my neck. Felt my cheeks heating up. "Um, hey. How's... How're you?"

"I'm coping. Still... still scares me. You know. How close we came to..." She shook her head. Smiled again. "How're you keeping?"

I wanted to tell Ellicia the truth. That the attack we'd survived was the least of my concerns and attention right now. I didn't want to lie to this girl. But I knew I had to do that to keep myself safe. To keep her safe. "I'm holding up," I said.

"You look... good."

My tongue felt heavy. I'd never been told that by a girl before. What the hell was I supposed to say in return? "Thanks," I managed.

There was silence between us for a few seconds, which dragged on, and I wondered whether thanking her for the compliment was the best way I could've gone about this when I had an urge to bring up the party. "Hey, I... After everything, it looks like I maybe might go maybe to the party maybe."

Ellicia's smile widened. Maybe might go maybe maybe? What the hell was I thinking?

"That's good," Ellicia said. "You know, I was thinking about not bothering. Might just kick back at home. Get a few pizzas. If you..."

She didn't say anything else. Just lowered her head. Looked at the ground. I sensed that she wanted me to ask her something, or say something, but the truth was I was still struggling to accept I'd just admitted I was going to the party. I didn't know what to say. Not one bit. Just that I had to *ask* her. I had to ask her to come to the party with me.

"Oh. Well, I, erm. Maybe I—"

That was all I managed.

I felt a nudge in my back.

I was pleased for the interruption until I saw who it was.

Mike Beacon towered over me. There was a different look in his eyes, though. He wasn't looking at me like he usually did. Neither were his two friends behind him. He was looking at me with a flat smile. Nodding his head. "Hey, Kyle," he said.

I wasn't sure I'd ever heard Mike Beacon ever say the words, "Hey, Kyle." What a weird day this was turning out to be. "Um, hey," I said.

Mike Beacon scratched the back of his neck. "Listen, man. What happened. At the soccer stadium. That shit was rough." He let that hang. "Guess I just wanted to say I'm glad you're back."

Mike Beacon didn't look me in the eyes, but I could feel myself smiling. Mike was actually drawing a line under the shit that'd happened between him and me. No, his bullying. That's what it was, no matter how I dressed it up. Bullying.

"That's cool," I said, pretending it wasn't that big a deal to me. "Thanks. I guess."

Mike nodded. He went to turn around. And then he stopped. "Oh, there was somethin', though."

He pulled his phone out of his pocket. Tapped on it a few times.

And then he swung it right into my face so fast I had to step back to avoid it hitting my nose.

"Looks like you're famous again, shitty-ass!"

I heard Mike and his friends laughing. But all I could see, all I could feel, was that video playing in front of me.

It was footage on YouTube. Footage from the attack.

And there I was. Standing still in the crowd.

Bottom lip poking out, like a little baby.

Tears rolling down my cheeks.

"That look!" Mike said, laughing. "Just look at that little baby face there!"

I listened to them laughing and felt the anger and the embarrassment building within.

I looked past the video at Mike. I looked at his neck. I pictured myself tightening my grip around it. Pictured myself punching him. Hard.

The video started to blur.

The phone dropped from his hands.

Smashed against the ground.

He turned and looked at it, and I knew I wouldn't be able to control my anger anymore.

I felt the tingling take over my body and went to pull back my fist.

"You evil shit!"

It wasn't me that said those words.

It was Ellicia.

She stepped around me. Slapped Mike Beacon across the face, silencing his laughing right away.

"After everything we went through, after the things we saw... how dare you. How dare you."

Mike Beacon clutched his cheek. Ellicia disappeared back to her friends, tears in her eyes.

"What?" Mike said, looking at me, red-faced.

I wanted to tell him what. I wanted to *show* him what.

But I knew I couldn't.

If Mike Beacon saw what I was capable of, my world would be over.

If *anyone* saw what I was capable of, my world would be over.

So I let Mike Beacon walk away. I held back, once again.

But I could feel myself getting closer and closer to snapping.

It wouldn't be long until I did.

It wouldn't be long until I *had* to.

15

I wasn't planning on playing around with my powers much after discovering I had them. Honestly.

But for some reason, I found myself walking to Dad's garage again later that night, the anger of the incident with Mike Beacon earlier welling up inside.

It was dryer tonight at least, so Dad wouldn't be down here checking on the dodgy roof at Peters' Parts. I'd managed to work out that was why he went there in the first place. He said he was planning on heading back down here to sort the dodgy window out at some point, but he'd been very hush-hush about it all. Didn't want to go into too much information. I knew I had to hurry. I didn't have long to play with my powers.

I'd got lucky in front of Dad once. Again? I'd been way too lucky overall lately. I wasn't going to take any chances.

I saw the garage up ahead and felt relief. I was a little bloated after just eating pizza back at home, and the taste of it kind of made me want to throw up when combined with the excitement I felt about trying out my powers again. It was strange, really. As much as I didn't want to use my powers in public, I needed a release. Kind of like masturbation. I was just playing around. Bringing myself to the brink.

And, well. Public masturbation was never a good idea. I might be pretty closeted from the naughtiness of the world, but I knew that much.

Much to my parents' relief, I gathered.

Just a loser. Not a public jerk-off loser. The lesser of two evils.

I crossed the road toward the garage and looked around. Pretty empty once again. In the distance, I could hear the sound of a boat blowing its horn, coming in from Manhattan. Over the sea on Manhattan, you could genuinely hear the chatter even though it was far away. It was like the city was alive. That's one thing that made New York unlike any other city on earth. I supposed I should be grateful, but I was kinda glad to be growing up in the forgotten cousin area over the water.

I was about to vault over the fence when I heard a scream to my right.

"No, please! Please don't—Please!"

I saw the woman standing by the ATM. She was wearing a brown cashmere coat. Two masked men surrounded her. One of them was holding her back. The other was trying to snatch her leather handbag away from her.

I felt the mixture of emotions build up inside as I witnessed this mugging. Part of me wanted to go over there. To help this woman. I had the power to do so, so what right did I have to just leave her to be robbed?

But on the other hand, I was afraid.

I was afraid that I'd be spotted. That my powers would be publicly known.

More than anything, I was afraid that I'd been lucky up to now. That I'd been on a lucky streak with my powers, and it was only a matter of time before they got the better of me, failed me.

"That—that necklace. My mom gave it me. Please... take everything. Just not... Just not..."

I saw the man in front snatch the necklace from the woman's neck. The man behind her laughed, then leaned in and kissed her.

I felt it inside me right then. Felt that spark, right up my spine, up the back of my neck.

This woman. I couldn't just leave her to be robbed. I couldn't let these men take something precious away from her.

So I pulled my black hood up. Pulled it right over my eyes.

I felt all the anger I'd ever felt inside. I felt all the pain tingling in my body.

And then I hurtled down the street towards the scene of the robbery.

The angrier I got, the more scared and uncertain I got of what I was doing, the faster I seemed to be moving. My legs were so fast that they were a blur. Within seconds, I was right next to the robbers, to the woman.

One of the robbers—the one who'd been holding the woman by her neck—looked at me. "What—"

I smashed my fist into his jaw.

I couldn't believe the force I'd caused with my bare hand. The man's jaw cracked out of its socket. His head went flying to one side. His entire body smashed into the wall that the ATM was built into. He fell to the ground and went still.

I breathed heavily. I was still stunned at what I'd done. I'd punched a man with the force to knock a wall down... and my knuckles weren't even hurting.

I looked up. Saw the woman staring at me, mouth wide.

And then I saw the second attacker running away, the woman's necklace and bag in his hand.

"Please. I—"

"Don't worry," I said, suddenly aware of just how undisguised I was, how exposed I was. I adjusted my hood. Made sure it was completely covering my face. "I'll get your things back."

I forced that anger and upset from my past to resurface and then I ran after the second assailant.

I could feel the power in every single step as I rushed towards the man. I felt myself getting to grips with the powers. Scarier than anything, I could feel myself getting more comfortable with them. I was an ULTRA. There was no denying that. And no ULTRA should be getting comfortable with their powers. Not in this world.

But I was doing a good thing.

I was using my powers for good. To help a woman in the street.

And more than that—I, Kyle Peters, was using my*self* for good. I was doing something brave. Something batshit crazy.

When could I ever say I'd done a thing like this in my life before?

I smacked into the second robber's back. It didn't take much to knock him down. I twisted him around with my mind. Pulled back my fist.

"Please!" the robber said. He held up his hands. Blood trickled from his lips. "Just—just take 'em. Take 'em!"

He held the bag and the necklace in my direction. His face mask had ripped so I could see that he was just a person. Just a terrified human being who'd done a bad thing.

"Don't ever let me see you around here again," I said. My voice sounded deeper. More assertive. Damn, I actually sounded *cool*.

"I won't," the man said. "Don't you worry about that."

I lowered my fist and I stood. The man got up soon after, and he limped off down the quiet street, looking over his shoulder to check I wasn't chasing.

I waited 'til he was out of sight, then I picked up the handbag and the necklace.

I ran back to the woman's side. Held the handbag and the necklace out to her.

"My necklace," she said. She was half smiling, half sad. "It's... He broke it."

I wanted to put it back together. I knew I could. I had the ability to do it if I tried really hard.

But I couldn't make myself look any more ULTRA. I couldn't make this woman suspicious.

"Thank you," she said. She looked me in my eyes. "Thank you so much. What's your..."

Before she could finish the question, I was already halfway down the street.

I couldn't deny I felt good. I couldn't deny I'd done something amazing. Something more amazing than I'd done in my entire life.

If only I knew right then that I'd made my first major error.

16

The following day, I couldn't help walking through school with a spring in my step.

It started when we were in history class. The sun shone brightly through the window, making it warm and stuffy inside. The smell of sweat from my fellow students was strong. It was usually a smell that made me feel ill. A smell combined with the hunger as lunchtime approached that tipped me over the threshold into nauseousness.

But not today.

I heard the three girls chatting about him first. The "mystery hero" who rescued a woman at a cashpoint last night. I heard one of the girls—Kayla Welsh, a pretty and moderately popular blonde—giggling. The hero had a positive image. I could live with this kind of attention.

And now I was outside, walking past the field with Damon. He was saying things to me. Going on about some video game or other. But I wasn't really taking it in. I wasn't really listening. I was just thinking about Ellicia and whether she meant what she said about me. Of course, nobody *knew* it was me. Fortunately, the hood blocked my face, and I'd been wearing pretty neutral clothing—natural for me. I'd also been moving pretty quick. Mainly, though, I was surprised just how human I'd seemed in that footage. I was worried I'd be exposed as an ULTRA all night.

But there was nothing to indicate it was me. Nothing.

At least, it didn't seem that way.

"Besides, I really like the donut place," Damon muttered, halfway through a bagel. "Don't see why they have to go closing it. Whaddya think? Kyle? Are you even listening?"

I wasn't. I found myself stopping. Standing and staring over at the field. Mike Beacon and his friends were playing football there. It looked a very private, exclusive affair, cool kids only. A few pretty girls were watching, and Mike was giving them that look he always did.

"Kyle? Umm.. you having nasty flashbacks or something, man? 'Cause the game's all done with now. You're not fake-shitting yourself anymore. Come on, let's get outta here."

But I didn't want to. I felt the anger building up inside. The anger I'd felt towards Mike when he'd mocked the footage of me in the midst of a gunman attack. The anger I'd felt when he mocked me for the shit incident, and the anger I'd felt for all the bullying over the last few years.

I felt the tingling up the back of my neck and an urge built within.

Could I?

It was dangerous. It was reckless. But...

"Hold this," I said.

I handed my rucksack to Damon and ran across the yard towards the field. I didn't even think about what I was doing. If I took a moment to think, I knew I'd probably legitimately shit myself.

"Kyle!" Damon shouted. "You got a death wish or something? You take a knock to the head?"

"Something like that," I muttered under my breath.

But nothing was stopping me. I kept on running in the direction of the field, in the direction of Mike Beacon's football game.

I saw a few of the players glance around at me as I approached. A few of the girls watching the game pointed and laughed. Mike Beacon hadn't seen me, though. He was running around with the ball in his hands, trying to get someone to catch him, but they just couldn't.

Eventually, he threw the ball. Not quite in my direction, but close enough for what I was about to do next.

I felt the anger inside me.

Felt the tingling fill my body.

And I hurtled towards the ball.

In a split second, I felt the ball land in my hands. I suddenly became aware of myself—Kyle, not the ULTRA Kyle —and I asked the same question in my mind that Mike Beacon asked when he finally turned and saw me holding onto the ball.

"What the hell you think you're doin', squirt?"

I stood there and felt my legs begin to shake. Mike stared intently into my eyes. He'd looked at me that way so many times before, and when he had, it was always when he was preparing to do something to torment me, to intimidate me.

But that wasn't happening again. I wasn't allowing it to happen again.

"You want the ball?"

Mike narrowed his eyes some more. I could feel the whispers surrounding me, the warmth of the sun burning my skin.

"Unless you want me to come get it," Mike said.

I saw a few smiles then. And I knew what Mike friends thought. I was just gonna give in. I was gonna give the ball back. They saw me for who I really was.

Only they didn't know who I *really* was. Not anymore.

I swallowed a lump in my throat and I held the ball tighter. "Come on then," I said. "Come get it."

I heard some whoops. Saw some claps. Mike Beacon smiled, but I could see his cheeks were red.

"Suit yourself, kiddo," he said.

He started to walk in my direction. Towering above me. Muscles twice my size.

I waited for Mike to step within a meter of me before I held the ball out.

Mike reached out for it.

Had his hands centimeters, millimeters, from grabbing it.

And I pulled the ball back and ran around the back of him.

I saw a few wide eyes as Mike tumbled forward. A few uncertain laughs. My heart pounded. By the side of the field, I could see Damon looking on, open mouthed.

"Come on," I said. "Thought you told me you wanted it?"

Mike turned around and I saw his face was completely red. There was no joy there, not anymore. "Don't test me, dick."

He lunged towards me.

I jumped up. Felt that tingling in my mind and jumped right over Mike.

I landed behind him.

Mike fell face flat into the grass.

I heard the laughter then and knew I couldn't take my powers much further. I'd just about got away with what I'd used without it looking too obvious. I had to give up. At least Mike wouldn't bother me now I'd shown him up.

I dropped the ball. "Here. All yours. Not my sport anyway."

I turned around and started to walk, feeling on cloud nine, on top of the world. I swore the pretty girls at the side of the field were even watching me.

When I felt the sharp pain in my left kidney, I realized they weren't looking at me at all.

Mike punched me to the ground. He knocked the wind right out of my body. I hit the grass with force. Because it was so warm, it was like hitting solid ground.

Mike turned me around. His eyes were bloodshot. "Don't you turn your back on me," he said. "Don't you dare turn your back on me, you little shit. Just 'cause you got caught up in a gunman attack, you think you're a hard-ass all of a sudden. Just 'cause you lost your sister all those years ago, you think you're above me. Just 'cause you've been through somethin' I haven't, you think I should fall in line."

When he mentioned my sister, in that split second as his fist hurtled towards my face, I wanted to keep my calm. I didn't want to use my powers again.

But the mention of my sister was enough to make me angry.

I stopped his fist. Twisted his wrist around. I pushed him back and sat atop him, flipping over his strong body with forces I was still amazed to have.

I focused on his neck. Tightened my grip, not using my hands but my mind. Tighter, tighter. And as I held Mike down, I could hear a few laughs at first. And then I could hear a few shouts. Voices right beside me. People saying something was happening to him.

All I could do was look down into the eyes of my tormentor as his face turned red.

Then purple.

Then blue.

And as I looked into his eyes, I knew that I was the one causing him this pain. I knew I was the one choking him.

And I didn't feel bad. I didn't feel anything.

I just felt angry at him.

I saw a tear roll down Mike's cheek. Heard someone by Mike's side asking if he was okay. And as I saw the tears, as much as I wanted to hold on with my mind's grip, I let go.

I let go and heard Mike wheeze for breath. Heard him splutter.

I stepped away from him, shaking. Stepped away as some more people from the school ran towards him. And as I stared at Mike Beacon choking, I understood the danger of what I'd done.

I'd used my powers. I'd used my powers to cover up the fact I was a wuss.

But I was still a wuss. Underneath, I was clearly still a wuss, because I was using my powers—not my own strength—to get one over someone who'd made a few jibes at me over my life.

I turned around. Walked away. I knew right then I had to be careful. Much more careful.

If it wasn't already too late.

HE WATCHED Kyle Peters closely from the other side of the field.

He saw the chaos. Saw the panic. Heard Mike Beacon coughing up his lungs.

But more than anything, more than anyone, he saw Kyle Peters.

At first, he wondered if he was the only one. But then he'd seen the footage last night, and he swore he recognized the shape of that hooded figure who saved the woman at the ATM. He'd always been good at recognizing people from their bodies just as well as their faces. But since discovering his powers, those abilities had tuned even more.

He wasn't totally certain if he was right. But he had a feeling. First, the gunman attack at the stadium. Then the events at the ATM. Now, this.

He couldn't be absolutely certain, but he'd be watching Kyle Peters very closely.

He thought he was the last one left.

Now, he knew he wasn't.

Now, he knew he didn't have to be alone. Never again.

He felt the tingling spread across his body and he forced his invisibility a little longer before disappearing out of the school grounds.

Kyle Peters was worth keeping a close eye on.

But for now, he had more important work to do.

17

"I mean, seriously man. I don't know what the hell got into you. But whatever got into you... Let it get into you again."

I sat at Avi's house playing video games, which had pretty much become a ritual on Wednesday evenings. My eyes stung with tiredness—the discoveries and whirlwind of the last week or so finally building up. My ears rang with the laughter of Damon, with the echoes of his voice telling Avi all about what happened with Mike Beacon on the football field earlier that day. So many people had come up to me, told me I'd done a good job standing up to Beacon—even his friends.

But I could smell the pizza Avi's mom was cooking downstairs and it brought a sour taste to my mouth, as delicious as it no doubt would be. I felt nervy. Constantly on edge. Even though I should've been on top of the world, I was on edge.

"Shouldn't gloat about it," I said. "Mike was in... He was in a pretty bad way when I left."

"Ah, screw him. That was his asthma. His own fault for getting so big on humiliating you if you ask me."

I nodded. Sipped back some Coke, which had gone flat. I

had to agree with Damon in public, but deep down I knew it wasn't true. I'd caused that "asthma attack". What happened to Mike Beacon was on me.

And it was that look in Mike's eyes—that human look of fear —that convinced me I had to hide my powers. I couldn't embrace them. Not even if I wanted to.

And I kind of really wanted to.

"Anyway, balls of steel," Avi said. "How's the chick?"

I frowned. "The chick."

"Yeah, you know. The chick. The one you been fawning over for like thirty years."

"Bit of an exaggeration."

"Only slightly."

I couldn't really argue with Avi on that front.

"So go on. Damon tells me you two've been hitting it off real good lately."

"He has, has he?" I glared at Damon. I wished Ellicia and I *had* been hitting it off. I mean, I wouldn't know if we had. Had we? We'd spoken a couple more times lately than we used to. But hitting it off? That was probably taking things a bit too far.

"Don't mind me," I said. "How about you and your girl?"

Avi shrugged. "Oh, Miri. Yeah, we're not together anymore."

"Sorry to hear that."

"It's cool. I'm hooking up with someone else now."

I almost spat my Coke out. "You... You don't speak to a girl in your entire life and all of a sudden you're seeing two in the space of a week?"

"It's that book," Avi said. "Told you it was gold."

"Yeah. Right."

"4.6 stars. Don't knock it 'til you've read it, bro."

I thought about what Avi had said about us "hitting it off." Honestly, there had been a few signs between Ellicia and me lately. There'd been the disappointment when I said I wasn't going to the party. And then when I mentioned I might be going, after all, it was as if she was looking for someone to ask her. Looking for someone to invite her along.

I thought about what happened with Mike Beacon on the field. That wasn't me, Kyle Peters. That was my powers. That wasn't me being strong. That was me using a weapon, just like any bully using a weapon.

The real person who needed to be strong? Me.

And I couldn't think of a better way to show just how strong I was getting.

I pulled out my phone as the sounds of the video games rumbled in the background. I opened up Facebook. Tapped on Ellicia—something I'd admittedly done in my more private moments. I hovered over the message screen. Wondered what I was doing. But maybe the best thing would be to not wonder at all. Maybe the best thing would be to just exit it. Just leave it. Just...

Hey :)

I felt my stomach turn to mush. The whole room around me disappeared into nothing.

Ellicia had messaged me.

She'd said "hey" to me.

Hey and a damned smiley!

I held a nervous finger over the message area. I thought about asking Avi for girl advice, but then I remembered I wasn't completely insane.

Just follow your feelings. That's what I'd heard was the right thing to do. Just do what I felt was right.

I typed in "Hi."

It looked too square. Too formal.

So I went for: "Hellloooooo!"

Felt like an idiot seconds later. Deleted it.

In the end, I closed my eyes. Thought about what I really wanted to say. Deep down, underneath all my fears, I thought about what words came most natural to me. I'd been through hell the last few days. This was nothing compared to being held up by a gunman.

Right?

I felt my phone buzz before I had the chance to respond.

Going to the party after all. Hopefully see you there. X

When I saw that kiss at the end, I couldn't help a cheeky laugh sneaking out.

Avi and Damon looked around. Avi's eyes narrowed. "The hell kind of laugh was that?"

I lowered my phone. Felt my body fill with the most joy it'd filled with since God knows when. "Looks like I'm going to the party after all," I said.

18

Daniel Septer hovered over his house and felt the power of anger within.

The night sky was jet black. There was a chill in the air, but it didn't matter to Daniel. He could feel warmth with the click of his fingers. The only thing that mattered to Daniel was the power he felt inside. The fury he felt inside.

The strength he'd been missing out on all his life, all of it swirling around inside.

He looked out over Manhattan Island. He saw all the lights, heard all the voices as if he was walking through the streets. Tourists. Businessmen. Taxi drivers. All going about their lives like everything was okay. All living their perfect little existences without a worry in the world. Making love to one another. Filth. Vermin. That's what they were. That's what they always would be.

All because of the way they'd trodden him down like he was nothing his entire life.

He tasted bitterness in his mouth as the memories of watching what happened to his stepdad, Garth, circled his mind. He'd thought about that a lot lately. Thought about the look on Garth's face as he hit himself with his own fist, again and again. Thought about the fear and confusion in his mom's eyes.

But that was the thing. Garth was gone now. Garth wasn't hurting anyone else, ever again.

Daniel had made sure of that.

For the first time in his life, he'd been the one to put a bully in their place.

He felt the anger tingling at his hot skin as he kept on hovering above his house. Mom was inside. He hadn't meant to lock her away in the basement, but she was just so eager to call the police about what happened to Garth. So keen to report it. He couldn't have that. Not at all.

Eventually, she'd come round. She'd see sense.

Right now, she was right where she needed to be.

Nobody would hear her scream.

He loved her so much.

He could hear people below, on the streets, but he knew it didn't matter. He was invisible. Nobody could see him. He'd been invisible in another sense for years already. Nobody paid any attention to him. Nobody took him seriously. And when he did attract attention, it was always the wrong kind.

Not again. Not anymore. Not after he finished.

He thought about all the kids that had trodden him down. Thought of the school bullies and their normal lives. Thought about the teachers, the moms and dads, all of them living their worry-free existences. They were ungrateful, that's what it was. When the ULTRAs were around, the world had a purpose again. A godless world had a vision of a God-filled future.

And humans had just taken that away again, infested the world, spread their venom further.

Really, the Era of the ULTRAs should've been a lesson. A lesson to appreciate life. To be kind to others. But the problem with humans was their memories. They were short term. One day, they could be in the midst of a terror attack, the next day they'd be out in a public place again like everything was okay, like nothing had happened.

Humans thought they were the gods. They thought they could defeat anyone. Anything.

But they couldn't. Because people like Daniel Septer were the gods.

People like Daniel Septer were going to rule this world.

People were going to fall to their knees for the ULTRAs once more.

Daniel looked over at Staten Island High School and he felt the anger tingling inside. The times he'd been punched. The times he'd had his money, clothes, everything stolen. The times he'd been given poor grades. He was going to make them pay. He was going to show them what it felt like to feel worthless. Powerless.

He was going to make them understand, and he was going to enjoy it.

And nobody was going to stop him.

Because nobody was powerful enough to stop him.

He thought back to Saint, and the chaos he'd caused—the explosions in Tokyo, the fires of Berlin. He thought of Saint swooping through the city of London, smashing every banker building in his wake. He saw the London Eye fall, the people inside it slip into the Thames.

And Daniel didn't feel the disgust that most people felt about Saint. After all, Saint wasn't the villain. It wasn't as simple as that; as black and white as that. Saint just wanted the world to be a better place. He wanted to free the world from the bully governments. He wanted to lead humanity into a new era—an era where the ULTRAs were the governments, the gods, and the people below served. Sure, he wanted people to fear him. What was any good leader if their people didn't fear him? That explained the explosions. That justified the killings.

But more than anything, Saint just wanted an end to the old ways. The narrow-minded human ways that had gripped the world like a disease for decades. Capitalism. Materialism. Mass population.

Saint wanted to rescue people from themselves.

But Daniel didn't want that.

He wanted the power. The control of a god. He wanted people to fear him.

But unlike Saint, he didn't want people to be saved.

He wanted people to burn.

And they would. They would. That day was coming. It was approaching. Fast.

Daniel dropped onto his house roof and lowered his invisibility. He looked out at the city, then back at Staten Island.

He would master his powers. The powers that he had been blessed with for a reason.

And when he did, he would tread everyone down.

The more he killed, the stronger he would feel. The more he destroyed, the more he would be feared.

Finally, he was standing up to the things that had made his life hell.

People.

He pulled down his dark silver metal mask, which he'd forced someone just outside the city to weld in a very comprehensive way, and to a very tight schedule. He made himself reappear from invisibility, just for a moment, and scanned his body. That armor. That silver metal armor. Again, welded by the best the city had to offer. He'd thanked the person who did it in his own special way.

Better than Saint's. Stronger than Saint's.

He took a deep breath from under that mask. Felt the power it gave him. The confidence it instilled in him.

He was starting a legacy of his own.

A new Era of the ULTRAs.

Daniel Septer was dead. Nycto was born.

He opened up the flyer to his school party.

He felt the anger at all the excitement around it, all the positivity around it. All the joy of people who'd punished him. People who'd treated him like hell.

The flyer started to burn in his hands.

He let it drop to the ground below.

And then he disappeared into the night.

Soon, the people who had made him suffer would feel pain themselves.

Soon.

He hoped Kyle Peters would be there to see the fireworks.

19

I looked in the mirror at myself and wanted to puke.

It was Friday night. Which meant one thing: party night. A matter of days ago, I honestly hadn't thought much of this night. I think I planned on staying at home, getting takeaway pizza, playing video games or watching Netflix or both.

But here I was, staring at myself in a mirror... Suited and booted.

My suit was all black. It was a pretty tight fit, which probably wasn't good news seeing as I was a five foot six rake as it was. I'd bought the suit with my own savings, though. Not in an actual suit shop, like Damon recommended—I wasn't fully out of the realms of total recluse just yet. I'd gone online and bought one that I thought would fit me.

Yeah. There wasn't a lot of time to send it back now. And it'd cost a lot of money.

But if it meant looking moderately good rather than... Well, not attending the party at all, then that's all that mattered.

'Cause Ellicia was going, and I had someone to impress.

I heard pots and pans downstairs. The sound of the television in the living room. The knowledge that my parents were just in other rooms while I was dressed ready for a party they didn't even know was on, let alone that I was attending it, made my stomach turn. I'd have to be quiet when I left. I'd have to make sure I got out without them seeing me. Maybe I could use my ULTRA powers to...

No. No using my ULTRA powers. There were a time and a place for my ULTRA powers, and that time and place was no time and no place. It was too risky. Too dangerous. I'd used them too publicly as it was.

No, I needed to work on my own problems. I needed to start being more confident in myself, not falling back on my powers to do the job.

And that started tonight.

That started with the party.

I pulled my phone out of my pocket. Part of me just wanted to take off my suit and hide in bed. I felt my heart racing every time I pictured myself in a hall filled with people I detested. What the hell was I doing? Why in God's hell was I attending this thing?

And then I saw Ellicia's Facebook posts and felt a different sort of tingling.

She was with a couple of friends at one of their places before the party. They were all dressed up, but my jaw dropped when I saw Ellicia. She was wearing a light blue dress. Her dark hair was curly and hung down on her shoulders. She wasn't plastered with makeup—she had a little something around her eyes—how was I supposed to know what it was? But she looked better for it. She still looked herself. Like the Ellicia I knew and... Damn, the Ellicia I loved.

She looked beautiful.

I opened up Messenger and tapped on her name, unable to shake myself from the moment.

On my way soon, I typed.

I hovered a thumb over it. If I sent this, there'd be no going back. If I sent this, I—

My thumb shook so hard that I accidentally tapped on the Send button.

And I realized I'd caught a wink-faced emoji before sending, too.

Dammit. No going back now. No going back.

Almost instantly after sending it, the message marked as read. And then Ellicia started typing. I could hardly contain my excitement and my fear. I couldn't believe this was actually happening—that I'd be as lucky as I was right now.

She sent back a single :).

When I looked back up at the mirror, I saw something poking against my ultra-tight black pants.

Damn. Yeah. I'd... I'd have to keep *that* in check if I wanted to avoid being laughed at tonight. That'd be a start.

I brushed back my hair a little, no idea whether it was making me look better or worse than before. I took in a sharp breath through my nose. Smiled. "You can do this, Kyle. You can freaking do this."

When I turned around, I saw Mom and Dad standing outside my bedroom door.

My immediate worry was, naturally, about my receding semi, which I hoped they hadn't noticed. But then another fear started to build. The wide look in both of their eyes. The twitching of Mom's eyelids. That pale look on Dad's face, a look of surprise, of questioning. They weren't supposed to see me like this. They weren't supposed to know about tonight. I didn't want to explain to them I was going—I just wanted to go, I just wanted to—

"Kyle?" Mom said.

I knew right then there was no getting away, no escaping.

My cheeks flushed. My knees started to shake. "I... I can explain. Just a last minute thing. Just—I woulda told you but—"

"You look amazing, son."

Mom wrapped her arms around me and held me tight. Her warmth radiated through my body as she stroked my back.

"I'm so proud of you, Kyle. So proud."

I wasn't sure how to feel as I stood there, my mom holding me, telling me how proud of me she was. And Dad was still just standing by the door, staring over at me like he'd seen a ghost. I wondered why he was looking at me that way. What it meant.

But then something even stranger happened.

Dad walked over.

He put a hand on my shoulder. He didn't look me in the eyes. He just put his hand on my shoulder and squeezed it.

"That's my boy," he said. I could hear the shakiness in his voice. "My boy."

I felt a lump in my throat. Tears building in my eyes. I felt the pride of my parents—the pride at me stepping out of my comfort zone, of doing something I was terrified of doing.

I was going to the party. I didn't *want* to go to the party, but I was doing it. And I didn't need superpowers to do that. I just needed my own powers. My own strength.

I let go of Mom, patted Dad back on the shoulder, and told them I wouldn't be too late.

"Don't you worry about being late," Mom said. "You have a special night. Then tell us all about it, okay?"

I wiped my eyes and nodded at Mom. I couldn't explain the emotion. Sadness. Happiness. A bit of both. "I will," I said. "I will."

"Goodbye, Son," Dad said.

"Goodbye, Dad."

He looked me in the eyes, just for the briefest of moments, and I couldn't quite figure out what that look was. Pride. That's what it felt like. For the first time in my life since Cassie died, my dad was proud of me.

I turned around before the tears had a chance to flow and disappeared out of my bedroom door, out of my house.

I didn't need any superpowers.

I just needed myself.

If only I knew what was ahead of me that evening.

Twenty minutes at the party and I hated it already.

I looked around at all these people I'd spent years of my school life growing up with. Very few of them I actually liked, and very few of them actually liked me. They were all suited, all looking trim and strong and muscular, all smiling at girls and looking like they were having the time of their lives.

I wished I could feel that way. And as I squeezed past these droves of people, the music thumping from the dance floor up ahead, I became increasingly aware of my own image. I thought I looked pretty sharp in my suit before I left. But now, seeing all these other people tailored and crafted to perfection? Now I wasn't sure.

My mouth was dry. I nodded at a few people that were vaguely familiar—people from my year who I never really spoke to. At least they weren't teasing me, pulling a practical joke on me. That made a change. I figured it had something to do with the events lately. The soccer game, the incident on the field with Mike Beacon.

Damn. I started to wonder if I was bordering on *cool*.

Just a shame I was finishing school for summer break soon. Ah well. Hopefully, the good word would follow me into next year.

The air was thick with the smell of aftershave. I didn't bother with aftershave, and in all honesty, I was glad I'd made that call now. It was smelly as hell as it was, no way anyone was gonna be able to tell I wasn't wearing any.

I searched around for my friends. Damon told me he was by the bar, which sounded way cooler before you saw it: the "bar" was just a little single-file line where a woman barely older than us handed out plastic cups of Coca-Cola. Not quite the bars you saw on movies. Which, in a way, I was kinda relieved about.

I squinted over at the dance floor, dared myself to look. Where the hell was Damon? He was supposed to be here. So too were some of our other mates—or rather, Damon's mates from classes—Paul, Chris, Sam. I got that awful feeling that maybe I'd been stood up. Maybe this was all some kind of prank from Damon to get me to go to the party. I'd made the bold call of turning up alone in the first place, without a grand photo entry.

Ah well. At least I knew Ellicia was here.

My stomach turned when I thought about Ellicia. I thought back to her message. She'd said she was here with a little smiley. What was I supposed to do now? Message her again and ask where she was at? Wander up to her looking all cool asking if she wanted a non-alcoholic drink? I didn't know. I was clueless. How was I supposed to know how to go about these things?

I decided to grab myself a Coke. It'd kill a bit of time, at least. I got in the awfully polite line and waited there, wishing there was a way I could hydrate myself using my ULTRA abilities without having to wait here dying of thirst.

I was close to reaching the front of the line when I felt someone push me.

"Keep moving. Don't make a scene."

I was tempted to use the strength I knew I had inside me—physically, at least—to stand my ground. But I figured now wasn't the time to make a show of things.

I let myself get pushed away from the queue, past the bar, and into a little darkened corner out of sight of the majority of the party.

When I turned around, I saw Mike Beacon standing right up to my face.

He didn't look happy.

I thought about what I could say to try and diffuse the situation. I really thought he'd have learned to leave me alone by now. I started to raise my shaky hands. Half-smiled. "Mike, if this is about—"

Mike pushed me back against the wall. Trapped me between his arms.

"The hell do you think you're doing showing your face here?"

I wet my lips, then realized in hindsight how ridiculous that'd make me look. "It's the party. I can be here if I want to be. Kinda." Almost tough. Almost assertive. Almost.

Mike's eyes were bloodshot. His jaw was shaking at the sides. "You've got some nerve."

"What happened. The other day. It was... it was an accident, Mike. But I'm glad to see your asthma's not stopped you—"

Mike pushed me back. Only this time, he did it harder. So hard that the back of my head cracked against the wall, sent a fuzzy sensation splitting through my skull.

"About that, Peters. You'd better watch your step after what happened. You'd better watch it real closely. Not step outta line."

I chanced a cocky return that I knew I'd earned. "I'd say it's you who might wanna watch out. I roasted you with that football."

I knew I'd made a mistake the moment the words left my lips.

Mike pushed me back again. Only this time, instinctively, I stopped myself before my head could crack against the wall.

I saw Mike's smile twitch a little. Just a little. But there was a weird look in his eyes. Shit. Had he seen me resist hitting the wall? Had he seen me using my abilities, just for that split second?

No. I was being stupid. I was being paranoid. I was—

"Funny thing happened when I got to the hospital," Mike said. "My peak flow. Way of measuring asthma, y'know. It was fine. Better than ever, in fact. Docs said they couldn't understand how I'd had an asthma attack when my symptoms were pretty much non-existent."

I felt my mouth growing even drier. He knew. He knew something was off.

"I dunno what happened out there," Mike said, tightening his grip on my wrists, leaning close to my ear. "But I'd say you might wanna watch yourself, squirt. Because if you step outta line one more time, I'll make sure everyone knows about our little secret. Everyone."

When he pulled away from me and looked me in the eyes, I knew.

I knew that Mike Beacon—my enemy, my nemesis—was aware that I had abilities.

ULTRA abilities.

And he was going to use them against me.

I watched Mike walk away, smile on his face, and the world around me slipped back into the focus. The booming music. The smiles. The choking perfume and the heat from the people I'd never liked, who'd never liked me.

Mike was dangerous. I had to talk to him. I had to make sure he didn't tell anyone. Damn, he could be telling someone right now.

I rushed in the direction I'd seen Mike go. I pushed past people, knocked drinks over. I felt a few shoves in my back, heard a few moans aimed at me, but they didn't matter.

Mike was the only thing that mattered right now.

Finding him and stopping him from telling anyone what he knew was the only thing that...

My thoughts froze when I saw Ellicia in the middle of the dance floor.

She looked gorgeous. Like a 3D version of that photo she'd uploaded to Facebook beforehand. Because that's exactly what she was, dumbass.

I wanted to go up to her. I wanted to walk across the dance floor and tell her I was here. Hold her hands. Dance with her.

But I knew that wouldn't happen. Not anymore.

Because she was dancing with someone else.

Another guy.

She was looking into his eyes with a sparkling look to her own. Not shifting her vision from him. Laughing at his jokes.

I felt the tingling burning up the back of my neck. I wanted to end the music. I wanted to bring the roof off this place, end the fun. I wanted to destroy it.

And then I heard a voice in my head. A voice telling me not to be ridiculous. Destroy this place? That was scary. That was an abuse of power.

That was the very evil that the ULTRAs were renowned for.

I looked at the girl in the middle of the dance floor—the only reason I'd come to this stupid event, the only reason I'd psyched myself up, got dressed up like this for.

I looked at her in the arms of another guy.

She looked at me. I swear she looked at me, just for a split second.

But it was too late.

By that point, I was already leaving.

Before I did any damage that I knew I was capable of.

That I knew had been building up under the surface for years.

21

I walked away from the party feeling as stupid as I should've felt walking to it.

The moon shone brightly from the dark sky above. The air was cold, a chill to my breath, but I didn't feel cold. I felt anything but cold. Probably because my cheeks were still burning with anger. Shame. Embarrassment. Hell, a crazy cocktail of all three.

I'd gone to the party and Ellicia had been there with another guy.

I saw a bin up ahead. It was overspilling trash. Without even thinking, I watched it topple onto the pavement, spilling its contents out. I knew I'd used my powers on it. And I knew I was being stupid. But shit. What did it matter anymore? What did it matter now Mike Beacon knew I had ULTRA abilities? What did it matter when the only girl I cared about was seeing someone else?

I squeezed my jaw and tried not to think back to Ellicia's messages. She'd been fishing for me to ask her to the party all along. Okay, *I* didn't think it looked like that, but eventually, I came to believe it.

She'd seemed happy. Happy that I was attending. So what happened? What had I done wrong?

I felt a sickening feeling in my gut when I heard the laughter of a couple walking at the opposite side of the road. The woman's high heels clicked against the pavement. The guy held an arm around her waist. In truth, they weren't much older than me—five, six years—but it seemed a lifetime since I'd reach that point.

I kept on walking and thought back to Ellicia's messages, as much as I didn't want to. Was it possible she just wanted to be friends after all? Which was cool. I wasn't one of those guys who berated girls for not wanting to be with guys. That led to all kinds of trouble.

But still...

Was that all it was? Really?

I waited until I knew the couple at the opposite side of the road had definitely disappeared from sight.

And then I kicked another trash bin over with my mind.

As I walked down Victory Boulevard, I realized I didn't really care what happened to myself anymore. Because we were only as good as the things we had, the people around us. And I had jack shit around me. Sure, I had my friends. I had my parents. But I only dragged them down, especially with the added burden of my ULTRA abilities.

I pulled back my foot and kicked the curb. It hurt my foot, but it damaged the curb even more.

What did it matter if I used my abilities a little now? Mike Beacon was gonna expose me for who I was anyway. It was only a matter of time before he got sick of holding that information for himself and actually used to it wreck my life once and for all.

I could keep my abilities under wraps. I could.

But I knew even the slightest suspicion of ULTRA activity and the police would be right onto it. The ULTRAs were gone, sure. But the memories of their destruction were not. It'd linger in "collective consciousness" for eternity, the newsreaders often said.

The last bit of life I had left as a free man, I wasn't gonna spend it terrified of Mike Beacon. I wasn't gonna spend it hidden away in fear.

I was gonna use my powers.

I was gonna use what I had.

Upon thinking it, I heard something crumble across the street. It took me a few moments to realize that some traffic lights were falling down. I watched the bottom of them split away from the concrete, watched them rip out of the ground and hurtle towards the road below. And I didn't care. Not an inch of me cared.

I just wanted to tear shit up.

I just wanted to destroy things.

I didn't care how psycho or crazy that made me sound. I'd been waiting for a moment to wreak havoc for my entire life.

Or at least, my entire life since Cassie died.

I sent the traffic lights falling to the road. I smashed windows. I felt the anger bubbling stronger within, only the new image sparking my anger was the smile on Mike Beacon's face, the glow in Ellicia's eyes as someone else held her, someone who wasn't me.

I stomped onto the ground and watched the sidewalk split for meters into the distance.

I bit down so hard that I felt my teeth shift.

I let out a cry.

My voice was so loud that I startled myself. It set car alarms off. Punctured tires. It even shifted a few huge trash canisters, opened a few doors. Up the road, I saw a homeless guy pushing along a bundle of clothes in a huge basket. Only he wasn't anymore—the bundle was on the ground.

I knew when I saw house lights flickering on that I needed to get away from here. I'd been stupid. I'd drawn way too much attention to myself. Not that it mattered, sure, but I wanted more time. More time to... Oh, I dunno what. Just more time.

I was about to sprint back home—or at least as far away from here as I could get—when I saw something weird overhead.

There was something in the sky. I thought it was a plane at first. But no, it was too bright for a plane. A shooting star? Nah. Way too big. Unless the government was covering up an impending impact, of course, which I wouldn't put past them.

I watched this fireball move through the sky. And soon I became aware of more people looking out of their windows, looking up at the sky. I heard voices. Shrieks. I heard a few televisions inside those houses, a few people speculating that the thing in the sky had caused the alarms in the streets, the crazy things I'd caused.

I dunno what it was, but I got a real sense of dread inside me as I watched this... this *thing* move. And the dread linked right to Ellicia, and to Damon and my friends.

Because this thing was heading right over to the party venue.

And it looked like it was getting bigger the closer it got.

I ran down the street. Ran down it, holding my breath and activating my camo as well as I could—which wasn't easy while I was running. Hadn't quite mastered the art of movement and invisibility just yet.

I reached the end of the street and saw the party venue up ahead. Heard the music blaring from it. Saw figures inside, having fun.

I saw the thing in the sky overhead.

Only it wasn't moving anymore.

It was just hanging there. Hanging in the sky above the party venue.

I realized then. I understood what this was. What was happening. It didn't add up. It didn't make sense. But then, neither did I. I was inexplicable too. My powers couldn't be explained.

But there was one thing certain here.

The thing above the party venue wasn't a vehicle. It wasn't a meteor.

The thing above the party venue was human.

It was impossible to make out any facial features, anything like that. And suddenly, facial features seemed irrelevant, meaningless.

The figure above the party venue lowered down, and flames appeared in the middle of its hands.

It lifted its hands. Pulled back the fire.

When I saw what was about to happen, I was already too late.

The figure shot a series of fireballs right at the party venue.

I watched the moment of stillness, of silence, as those fireballs headed towards the venue. I watched them hurtle from the figure—the ULTRA's—hands, one after the other.

Eight of them.

Ten of them.

Twelve, sixteen, eighteen...

It felt like those fireballs hovered for so long that they were never going to hit.

But they did.

They blasted into the party venue.

Sent an explosion ripping across Staten Island.

And then another fireball hit. And another. And another.

I didn't hear music anymore. I didn't hear laughter. I didn't smell cheap aftershave.

I smelled burning.

I heard screams.

Screams, as more fireballs ravaged the party venue.

The venue where Damon was.

The venue where Ellicia was.

22

I wasn't sure how long I stood staring as my party venue was pummeled with fireballs.

The light from the flames lit up the night sky. The air was thick with the smell of burning. My ears rang from the sounds of the blasts—not just ringing from the actual blasts themselves, but the echoing they created around my head. I felt sick. Like I could throw up right here. My body was frozen to the spot.

There was another ULTRA. That's what I was witnessing. Another person with ULTRA abilities, just like I had.

And they were attacking my party venue.

I saw the chaos and for a split second, selfishness kicked in. I understood what this meant in a flash. I'd be hunted down. Hell, I might even be blamed for this.

But that momentary flash of worry, of concern, disappeared almost as quickly as it appeared in my mind.

Because I became aware that Damon and Ellicia were inside that party venue.

I wanted to run. I wanted to teleport myself back home and

bury my head under my pillow. I couldn't be seen out here. I definitely couldn't use my ULTRA abilities. It was reckless. Dangerous.

But then I heard the screams, and I pictured the fear that Damon, Ellicia, so many others must be feeling right now.

I knew I couldn't just leave my friends—leave Ellicia—in there. Not to burn. I couldn't just let them die. Not when I knew I had the capability to do something about it.

I ripped off my tie. Threw off my blazer. I thought about how to go about this. Obviously, I had to disguise my face a little. I couldn't just appear in there showing everyone my abilities.

No. I had to do something.

I ripped a strip of material from my blazer. In the distance, I heard more explosions. Shit. I had to stop dicking around. I needed to be quick.

I tore off some more of the blazer material, grimacing as I destroyed the most expensive piece of clothing I'd ever owned. I lifted it to my face. Tore a few eyeholes in the material.

I tied it around my face using my tie.

It wasn't the best look. Wasn't the most intimidating look.

But it was the disguise I needed right now.

I started to move quickly towards the party venue. Started to blaze my way towards it. And I heard that voice in my head again. The voice of the wuss I'd been all these years telling me I was an idiot, that I was being stupid and was going to get myself killed. That I should just go back home and let the police and the people in the know deal with this situation.

I agreed with the voice. I knew I had a fat chance of fighting off whoever was attacking the party venue.

But I wasn't going to give up on Damon and Ellicia that easily.

I had a duty to save them.

I sprinted towards the party venue. Sprinted across the streets, moving quicker than I'd ever moved before. Sometimes I didn't even have to run to lurch forward a few steps, like I was combining my teleportation with my super-speed. I wondered if that was how it worked—if I could only teleport short distances.

I'd have to figure that out another time. If I ever got out of this party venue.

I felt the heat from the flames getting hotter as I neared the party venue. In the distance, sirens. The police would be here soon. So too would the fire department. And whoever attacked this place seemed to have gone quiet, like their work was done.

But I wanted to know Damon and Ellicia were okay. If they were in here, surrounded by flames, I could spare their lives. I could save them.

I had to know they were okay. I just had to.

I stepped inside the door I'd walked out of not long ago. When I pushed it open, I felt that sickness inside getting stronger, creeping up my throat.

The party venue was in ruins. In tatters like I'd never seen a place before. There were people with their arms over each other's shoulders dragging themselves towards the door. People smeared with black marks, coughing up the thick dark smoke.

But the worst things I saw were the still people.

The people I recognized lying by the side of the corridor. Dressed in their suits. Dressed and ready for what was supposed to be the happiest night of their lives.

Motionless.

I didn't want to look at the motionless bodies, but I knew I had to. I held my breath as I checked every one, feeling terrible both about the deaths *and* the fact I felt relieved whenever I saw one of them wasn't Damon or Ellicia.

Where were they? Where the hell were they?

"Get... get out," I heard a voice say. A guy called Peter Barnes hobbled past me, towards the door. His shirt was covered in blood. "Get out."

I wanted to. I wanted to follow Pete out of that door and get the hell out of this place forever. Because this wasn't a party anymore. This was the scene of a crime. The scene of a *horror*.

But I had to know Ellicia and Damon were okay.

I held my breath and forced the camo, even though I wasn't sure how long I could hold it for. Kind of like holding in a piss when your bladder was absolutely bursting in the middle of a three-hour film in the cinema. Which had happened to me once during the Dark Knight, right from the scene where the Joker attacks the hospital.

This was harder. Way harder.

I pushed past a few people. Checked the bodies. I flew through the smoke and found myself coughing. For all my powers, it was a pity I couldn't find a way to stop the smoke filling my lungs. Or maybe I could stop it. Maybe I was already stopping it, filtering it. I didn't know. Right now, I wasn't sure how far my abilities went, what restrictions there were.

I ran a little further, past the bar, towards the dance floor. Despite the heat and the screams, I could still hear that music blaring, which gave the whole place an even creepier vibe.

Ellicia had been down on that dance floor. She'd been dancing with the guy I'd seen her with. She couldn't have gone far. I hadn't left long ago.

So where the hell was she? And where the hell was Damon all this time?

I reached the bottom of the steps to the dance floor and looked through the smoke, through the flames.

It was at that moment that I saw them.

Damon and Ellicia were close by. Really close by.

They were both lying down. Still.

Damon had a cut on his head. Ellicia was covered in a gray, dust-like substance.

I felt a knot lurching at my throat and flew over to them. I had to get them out. Had to get them away. Didn't care whether anyone saw me anymore. Didn't care whether I wasn't disguised or anything.

All that mattered was them.

All that mattered was that they were okay.

"Come on," I muttered, lifting Damon in my left arm, and then Ellicia in my right. I felt sad, making contact with her. Like it was something I shouldn't be doing. Like it should be her boyfriend's job.

He was nowhere to be seen. I had to worry for him.

I pulled Damon and Ellicia under my arms when I heard something split above.

I looked up and saw a pane of the roof flying down, right toward us.

I had a flash of it hitting me on the head. Of the flames and the smoke completely engulfing the three of us together.

And then it stopped.

It stopped, right in midair, and it flew across the room and blasted through a wall.

I wondered how that'd happened. I hadn't caused it. Unless my abilities were coming more fluidly, more natural, I definitely hadn't focused enough on that section of roof to send it through a wall.

It was then that I heard the shout.

It was a voice I recognized, over to my left. When I looked, eyes stinging from the smoke, I couldn't believe what I was looking at.

Mike Beacon was hovering above the ground. He was

pressed right up against the wall, clutching at his neck. There was fear in his eyes.

There was someone opposite him.

A man, no doubt. Dressed all in silver, like a knight from medieval times. The way he was dressed gave me the creeps. It reminded me so much of Saint, of how he used to dress when he terrorized the world for all that time.

Maybe he was back.

Maybe he was...

"Help! Please!"

Mike's shout snapped me out of the moment again. I saw the ULTRA hovering closer towards him. Saw him stretch out his hand and saw Mike's face go redder, just like when I'd been choking him during the football game. And a part of me felt awful because I knew Mike knew that I was an ULTRA. If he knew, then he could blame me for this. He'd seen me leave. He'd know, and he'd blame me, and I'd be punished for everything.

But no. I was being selfish. I was being stupid. Mike might've been a dick to me all my life, but he was just a guy in my year. He didn't deserve to die in here. He didn't deserve any of this.

I wanted to fly over. I knew I could knock the ULTRA off balance. I knew I could stop them.

But then something horrible happened in my moment of hesitation.

Something totally awful.

The ULTRA lifted Mike higher into the air.

Right through the roof. So high that he became invisible, just a dot in the sky.

And then the ULTRA lowered his hand.

Mike came crashing back down with immense force.

Disappeared into a crater in the ground.

The ULTRA turned around from the smoking crater. I swore he looked right across the dance floor, right into my eyes.

And then he disappeared off into the sky, disappeared into oblivion, as I held on to Damon and Ellicia's limp bodies and stared down at the crater that Mike Beacon had disappeared down.

23

I sat in the hospital for the second time in a week.

This time, I was here for completely different reasons.

I sat in the corridor outside the main ward. Nurses dressed all in white kept on walking by and smiling at me, clipboards in hand. Every now and then, patients stumbled past, some of them moving so sluggishly that I couldn't believe they were still on their feet. There were a constant chatter and a constant bleeping of machinery. The stench of disinfectant and sweat hung in the air. I'd eaten a burger before I made my way down here, and it wasn't settling well.

Nothing was.

Because my best friend and the girl I loved were the ones in the hospital beds, in a condition I didn't even know about.

I tried to hold my leg still, but it wouldn't stop shaking. I told myself they were okay. I'd felt their hearts beating when I'd got them to the hospital. They were lucky. I'd got them here and got rid of my makeshift outfit before everyone else had the chance to be brought here. Not that I was being selfish—there were a lot of injuries after the attack on the party venue. But my friends were at the front of the line for medical attention. To me, that mattered more than anything.

I'd rang Mom shortly after dropping Damon and Ellicia off. Told her I was fine. That I'd got away before the incident occurred. I called it an incident, but truth be told, I wasn't the only person who knew exactly what'd happened at the party. I could hear whisperings about it. I could feel the tension in the air; see the startled looks in the eyes of the nurses, the eyes of the terrified classmates who'd been brought in for a variety of wounds.

Even Mom mentioned it on the phone.

"Is it true, Kyle?" she'd asked. "The ULTRAs. Is it true that they're back? That they're really back?"

I heard the fear in my mom's voice, and even though there wasn't a thing I could do about my own powers and abilities, I felt ashamed of myself for having them. My mom hated the ULTRAs. She hated them for what they'd done. For the destruction they'd caused. But mostly, of course, for the death of my sister. Instead of blaming the governments who created the first wave, instead of blaming Saint for forcing Orion into a climactic showdown with him, she lashed out at the same target as everyone else—all the ULTRAs. Every ULTRA.

If she knew I was an ULTRA...

I shuddered at the thought. She'd be even more embarrassed by me, even more ashamed than she must've been already.

I wiped a finger across my head. There was a little blood there. It made it look like I'd been caught up in the attack. The truth was, I'd made it myself not long ago. I didn't have my story straight, not just yet. I hadn't decided whether to explain that I'd left literally moments before the attack or not, but then even though I was partly masked when I'd gone back into the party venue, I couldn't be too sure nobody had recognized me, or that CCTV would find a nifty way of picking me up.

I'd told Mom I was by the door when it happened. That I got out fine. She told me I had an angel looking out for me. My sister's angel. Surviving a mass gun attack; surviving an ULTRA attack on a school. An angel on my shoulder.

To me, it felt like a demon was inside me, shadowing my every move.

I knew there'd be questions. I knew I'd have to settle on a story. But right now, my brain wasn't working. All I wanted to know was how Damon and Ellicia were getting along. I'd heard talk about the death toll at the party venue already. At least ten. Not as bad as it could've been, but a lot of injuries. And ten too many. Ten preventable deaths.

I just hoped Damon and Ellicia didn't make up those numbers. I hoped they weren't gonna be crippled for life.

I'd never forgive myself. I should've been there. I shouldn't have let Mike Beacon's threats get to me. I was probably just being paranoid about those anyway. God, they seemed so superficial now.

I felt my body go cold when I thought back to the last time I'd seen Mike. I'd looked down into that crater in the ground; the crater that... well, whoever the other ULTRA was threw him into.

Smoke steamed from his body. He was still.

As much as I disliked the guy, I hoped he made it. 'Cause he was just a guy my age.

Not just that, but I felt guilty. I'd hesitated when I saw the ULTRA attacking Mike. When I saw him holding Mike up, strangling him. I'd actually questioned helping him. What kind of a Hero did that make me? Didn't that just make me the same morally screwed idiot as every other ULTRA that everyone feared?

I thought about that ULTRA dressed all in silver armor. Thought about the metal mask, so reminiscent of Saint's. What was their problem with the party? Why had they attacked the venue? High casualty targets were Saint's manifesto, sure. But a party venue on Staten Island for a relatively lesser-known high school? Surely that didn't totally fit in with Saint's modus operandi.

I knew right then, sat there, that I was in a dangerous world now. I was so far down the rabbit hole that I wasn't sure I'd ever get out again.

I'd hesitated. If I'd acted sooner, I could've stopped the ULTRA from causing more destruction, more chaos.

I was still the weak moron deep down that I'd always been.

I was about to stand up and see if I could find any news on Damon and Ellicia when I heard a voice to my left.

It was a doctor. A short, black woman, who I'd seen earlier when everything was still a little blurry.

"Kyle, right?" she asked.

I nodded. I felt my chest tighten. This was it. I imagined a zillion scenarios. A zillion different forms of bad news.

"Damon Bamford and Ellicia Williams. You were asking about them."

This was it. The bad news was coming. I was too late. I hadn't acted quick enough.

"They've got some minor burn wounds, a little concussion. Otherwise, they're absolutely fine."

I almost lost my footing. "Thank you," I exhaled. "Thank you so much. Can I... can I see them?"

"Their families are with 'em right now," the nurse said, starting to turn around. I could hear a cry from one of the other wards. She had to be so busy right now. "Give it an hour or so, I'm sure your friends can't wait to see you."

"Me too," I said. "Me too."

I watched the nurse walk away, and I felt like I was on cloud nine.

I went to sit down. Heard the crying some more. When I looked over to my right, I realized it wasn't a patient crying at all. It was a woman in a black coat. Tall. Blonde. Attractive. Beside her, her older husband, holding an arm around her. He looked like he'd seen a ghost.

Weird thing about them. They looked vaguely familiar. I swore I'd seen them somewhere before. I swore I'd...

Then, it clicked.

It clicked, and I felt all the heat leave my body.

I did recognize them. I'd seen them at parents' evenings. I'd even seen them around at my parents' house back in seventh grade when the bullying first started properly, as they attempted to put an end to it like adults did.

"I'm sorry, Mrs. Beacon," the bald doctor standing opposite said. "I'm so sorry. We tried everything for your son. But we just... I'm so sorry."

I didn't have to hear any words to confirm it.

Just the croakiness in the doctor's voice. The pain in Mrs. Beacon's cry.

Mike Beacon was dead.

24

"Seriously, man. The things I saw there. You... you wouldn't believe it. You missed out. Classic Kyle."

I stood beside Damon's and Ellicia's beds and felt sick right to my stomach. The ward had quietened down, and it didn't seem as rushed and panicked as it had earlier when the people caught up in the party attack were admitted in their droves.

But the sound of Mrs. Beacon's cries, her grief, didn't escape my mind.

The sound of those words from the doctor.

"I'm so sorry, Mrs. Beacon. We tried everything for your son. But we just... I'm so sorry."

"It's really shitty," Damon said. "I mean, I swear we're cursed or somethin'. Terror attack. Now this. One of us has to have broken a window or something."

"Broken a window?" Ellicia whispered.

"Yeah, y'know. Bad luck and all that."

"I think you mean a mirror," I said.

"What? Nah, man. I definitely mean a window."

"He really means a window," Ellicia said.

I nodded. I wanted to smile at Damon's silliness. He was always coming out with stuff like that. But truth be told, I couldn't laugh at anything. Yeah, I was pleased I'd been the one to drag the two people closest to me out from the wrath of the party venue. But so many others had suffered. People our age had *died*. There was something wrong about that. Something so damned wrong. As if the world had glitched like a video game and some terrible bug had crept in.

"It's kinda cool in a way," Damon said.

"What is?" I asked. I hadn't really looked at Ellicia much since stepping into this room. I couldn't face seeing the bloodied cut on her forehead and knowing that if I'd been here when the fireballs rained down on the venue, I could've stopped even more pain. If I hadn't walked away like a wuss, I could've fought.

But I hadn't. And now people were dead. People I cared about. People I didn't care so much about.

But still, people. People just like me, coming to the end of their school year, living normal lives.

"It's cool that there's... there's an ULTRA back," Damon said.

Ellicia tutted.

"What? Don't you think it's kinda cool?"

"In what way is an ULTRA being back 'cool'?" Ellicia snapped. She didn't snap much. In fact, I don't think I'd ever seen her angry before now. Seen the redness to her face.

But she was mad enough about the thought of an ULTRA being back that she was willing to let her peacefulness slip.

"They caused so much death. So much chaos. Hell, they even killed Kyle's sister."

I felt my skin turn cold.

Damon looked down at the bed.

"Sorry," Ellicia said. "I... I shouldn't have—"

"No," I said, feeling more deflated by the minute. "No, you're right. I just..."

"I'm just saying," Ellicia continued. "The ULTRAs. Yeah, they mighta been designed to protect us. But we only just made it. Every single one of us only just made it. People were never meant to have powers. It's just something that was never meant to happen. We got away with it. We got lucky. And now there's an ULTRA back... well, I just hope the world's ready again. 'Cause usually we don't get lucky twice."

I heard Ellicia's words echoing in my ears and knew there was desperation there. Desperation that had hung over everyone since the day of the Great Blast. The fear. The fear of "what if?" another ULTRA were to crop up someday. The government said it was impossible. That the fears were unfounded.

But what if?

I knew now it was true. An ULTRA was back.

Not just one. Two.

And I was one of them.

I decided to take my chances and test the waters. "Maybe if there's a bad ULTRA back, there might be... another. Another like Orion who can stop whoever it is."

Ellicia rolled her eyes. "Saint. Orion. They're all the same at the end of the day."

"I don't think that's true."

"You don't have to," she said. She looked me right in the eyes, tears building in the corners. "You only have to see all the destruction they caused trying to save the world in their own ways to know the truth."

More than ever before, I felt ashamed about my abilities. There was no winning Ellicia round to my side of the argument. Not that I'd been planning on telling her or anyone about what I was capable of in the first place—there were still so many things I didn't understand yet. But still, knowing the girl I loved didn't view what I was as a good thing, as a hero... that was pretty soul destroying.

"What happened to Mike," Damon said. "It's fucked up. I mean, I never liked the guy, but it's fucked up."

My throat was so dry that I couldn't speak. I nodded.

"I don't know how we got out that party venue," Damon said, shuffling around on his hospital bed. "I just know that whoever it was... well, they were the real hero in all this. The paramedics, whatever. They were the real hero."

I was the real hero. I wanted to say it aloud. I was the hero.

"But before I left. I saw... I saw that look in Mike's eyes. Just for a split second. He was scared, man. Like he knew. And that's what creeps me out so much about all this. Mike Beacon, the toughest guy in school, looking at me like I could help him somehow. Like he needed *my* help."

I felt the heat of the room intensifying around me as the memories flooded back.

I felt the guilt of failure building inside.

"Visiting time's over I'm afraid, kiddo," an approaching nurse said. She smiled at me, scrunched up her face. "Time for your friends to get some rest."

I said my goodbyes to Damon. I walked over to Ellicia's bedside, and as much as I wanted to hug her, I just held my hand up awkwardly, waved at her. She nodded back. Half-smiled. She looked tired, worn down, but still amazingly beautiful.

If only I could tell her. If only I had the guts to tell her.

I left the ward and headed back down the hospital corridor. As I walked, I saw people I recognized in the hospital beds. I saw anguished faces of parents. I saw tears.

And as I stepped past these people, I couldn't help feeling guilty that I was here, that I was okay.

But also, that I had failed.

One thing was for certain: if I hadn't been so in denial about my powers, maybe this wouldn't have happened.

But what could I do about it now?

25

"You sure you should be watching this, Kyle?"

I stared at the television in our living room back home. I hadn't goosed out and watched TV in what felt like forever. The living room was dark, lights out, like it always was whenever the TV was on. It was also turned down just below comfortable hearing, something Mom and Dad always insisted on 'cause they were worried about the neighbors. My lips felt dry and chapped. There was a constant sickly feeling hanging in my body, like the events—the discoveries—of the last few days were still weighing down on me.

I was an ULTRA.

There was another ULTRA attacking people. Killing people.

The world was changing right before my young eyes all over again.

"Turn this up," I said, when I saw the news report flash to an explosion in Cairo, Egypt. "Please."

Dad sighed. Then he reached for the remote and inched the volume up ever-so-slightly.

The report was about an explosion, as I'd noticed. But it

wasn't just any old explosion. There were those fireballs blasting down on the Cairo streets. Fireballs, just like the ones that had rained down on my party venue.

"And reports at the scene are suggesting an attack just like that at the school party on Staten Island. An ULTRA attack..."

I heard the fear in the newsreader's voice. I heard the collective gasps of air of everyone watching this breaking news unfold as if I was in each and every one of their living rooms.

I saw the fear on my mom and dad's faces. The same fear that'd been there the day my big sister died.

"There's also reports of a YouTube video from the attacker."

My ears pricked up.

"The legitimacy of it was in doubt at first, but now it appears to have been verified."

Dad lifted the remote. "Your mother doesn't need to hear this."

"No, wait," I said.

I saw Dad's finger hover over the remote, ready to change channel. I was so close to snapping the remote with my mind. But I had to keep my calm. I couldn't go giving away my secret identity to my parents. They'd probably disown me.

I didn't have to. Dad sighed, lowered the remote.

The news report changed to some clear footage, shaky but clear. Not the grainy type that is so clichéd in movies and television shows.

The ULTRA was just like the one I'd seen at the party venue. Dressed all in silver armor, like a knight. Wearing a metal mask over its face.

The ULTRA was hovering above the pyramids of Egypt.

"Humanity has been a scourge on the planet for way too long. Burning fossil fuels. Wasting the earth's natural resources. Fighting with one another. It's a virus that has gone beyond control. A virus where the powerful stomp down on the less powerful, and the less powerful who do find power just abuse it like their superiors. Because that's human nature. To destroy others.

"But it does not have to be that way much longer. It is time for somebody else to do the destroying. For something else to vet humanity's actions."

I saw the fireball appear above the ULTRA's free hand.

"I am Nycto. Night is coming."

He let go of the phone and it stayed there, hovered in the air.

The next thing I saw was Nycto raining down his fireballs on a hotel resort in Egypt.

The footage cut away. Seconds later, Dad changed the channel. A comedy came on, Family Guy. He smiled right away, started chuckling. But I could tell it was forced. How could anyone laugh anymore? How could anyone laugh when Nycto, had just declared war on humanity?

I pulled out my phone and scanned the news. I saw that close up of Nycto's mask again. Definitely the same guy I'd seen attack my party. What was he doing attacking Cairo? What was the link?

I scrolled down a little further. Saw there was a statement from President Marko.

"Nycto is dangerous. And he must be treated seriously. Humanity must come together to defeat this threat. To stand together, just like we stood together last time, and defeat Nycto."

There was a question. A reporter asking the president whether there was another ULTRA out there. One like Orion, who could take Nycto down just like Orion took Saint down.

"Let me be clear," the president continued. "We made a mistake creating the ULTRAs. And no ULTRA should be glorified. We have no reason to believe there are any other ULTRAs out there. But if there is, well..." He looked right into the camera. Looked into my eyes like he could see me in my living room. "Do the honorable, democratic thing. The American constitutional thing. Turn yourself in. That is the only way you can help us."

The recording cut out, and I was left with the president's words ringing in my ears.

I knew what President Marko was saying. I knew exactly what he was implying. If I gave myself up to the government, they'd end me. They'd make an example of me. At the very best, they'd use me. Weaponize me in their fight against Nycto.

But I was just a kid. Just a sixteen-year-old kid who didn't know how I'd got these powers; didn't know where they'd come from.

I didn't want to be weaponized. I didn't want to turn myself in. I hadn't done anything wrong.

I stood up, a sudden bolt of life shooting through my body. I felt a sense of purpose fill me. Life filled my lungs as the sounds of the screams, the memories of the flames, all of them filled my consciousness.

"Where're you going?" Mom asked.

I tightened my fist. Felt the electricity fill my body. "Nipping out," I said.

I couldn't just sit by and watch Nycto tear the world apart.

I couldn't let more people die.

I had to do something.

26

I stood in the garage and thought about the things that infuriated me most in life.

I watched the metal bar in front of me lift as I focused my mind on it. I could hear other things in the room clanging around me. Items I was lifting simultaneously along with the metal bar. Loose tires. Spare wheels. Tubs of paint, all of them rising through the power of thought.

I gritted my teeth, bit down so hard on my bottom lip that I tasted blood.

And when I tasted blood, I thought about the moment I'd lost my sister.

I felt the anger within. The anger and the sadness. And after I'd felt that, I saw the metal bar in front of me lift higher. I focused on bringing it towards me. Lifting it closer to my current position. The other items I was lifting around the garage all drifted towards me too; the light above flickered, and I felt a breeze.

I thought about Mike Beacon. Not just the times he'd bullied me, not just the times he'd tormented me, made my life a misery. But that moment when I discovered he was dead. The moment I *witnessed* his death.

Nycto holding him by the throat.

Then throwing him right down into the ground, slamming him into oblivion.

I heard Damon's words in my ears. The words he'd said about the fear in Mike's eyes. How Mike looked like he just wanted help from somewhere, from someone.

I knew I could've been the one to help. I knew I'd failed Mike Beacon.

I'd killed him.

And that just made the anger, the fury, the fear and the guilt, all of them build up inside me.

The metal bar flew towards me. So too did everything else.

I stopped them. Held them stationary in the air. They floated around me, drifted around in a circle. Heavy items. Metal. Wood. Parts of cars. All of them drifted around me like I was the sun and they were the planets.

I knew what I had to do. I had to learn to embrace my powers. I had to learn to use them. I couldn't turn myself in to the government. They'd never let me free, not once they'd finished with me.

No. I had to get to grips with my powers. Because right now, I knew I was the only person anywhere near capable of stopping Nycto.

I let out a shout and sent everything inside this garage hurtling towards the other sides of the room.

As they flew towards the walls, I used my strength to speed towards every item. To stop them, put them back in place before they damaged their surroundings. I grabbed metal vice grips. Grabbed old steering wheels. Stopped a tire from smashing through one of the windows. I kept on going. Kept on getting faster. Kept on using my speed and my pace and everything I had to make sure I didn't damage this garage.

When I stopped, I looked around. A few of my targets had hit. A few things had been smashed. So I'd practice. I'd do it again until I was absolutely sure I was stronger, quicker. Because yes, I was scared. I was afraid. But I had to embrace my powers or there'd be a lot more to be afraid about. I couldn't hide anymore. I had to use my powers.

I had to be someone.

Not an ULTRA. No.

I had to go back before the ULTRAs. I had to give people hope, just as they first had.

I had to be a Hero.

I realized I needed something. Something that all Heroes and ULTRAs had. A disguise of some kind. I thought about the movies. The superhero films, the DC classics. All of the heroes had a disguise. A costume.

I needed a look. I needed to give people hope.

I had work to do.

THREE HOURS LATER, I stared at myself in the mirror.

I was dressed head to toe in black. Tight black jeans. Black suede desert boots. A black turtle-neck top, tight fit. To look at me, I looked like a magician or someone dressed for a night out.

And then I lifted the black cotton mask and pulled it over my head.

I felt myself transform when that black mask covered my face. To look at me, you wouldn't know there were eye holes in the material, but I'd cut two tiny slots that allowed me to just about see. I felt warm. I felt like I was wearing a new skin. A second skin.

I wasn't Kyle anymore.

I was someone else.

Just one final touch.

I lifted the stitching I'd found at an old thrift store in New Jersey. I pressed it up to my chest, stuck it on.

When I'd attached it, I couldn't help smiling.

I was complete.

On my black chest, a circle. A dark planet with light beaming from around its sides. All around it, other little dots, little stars.

The very same image Orion used to wear.

The logo of hope.

I gawped at myself for a few more minutes before stepping away from the mirror. I felt self-conscious, but not as me, as Kyle. As my new self. As *Orion*.

But if I wanted to succeed, there were things I had to do.

Hope I had to restore.

As scary as it was, I had to draw attention to myself to show the public that there was another person with abilities, but that they weren't all bad. That in the darkness, there was hope.

I had to draw attention to myself. Positive attention.

And there was only one place to start.

27

Harry Carson stared into the large metal container and felt a smile tugging at the corners of his mouth.

It was freezing. Freezing as hell. Sure, might've been summer, but New York was no Los Angeles, that was for sure. Everything was different about this place—the weather, the buildings. I mean, the Empire State Building. They don't build 'em like that in California.

They didn't do drug operations like this in California, either.

The sounds echoed from the city. Sounds of nighttime partygoers, all going about their normal lives. The air was thick with the smell of sewerage and filth. The water splashed up against the side of the harbor, making the air seem even colder.

As much as Harry hated New York, hated his visits to this godforsaken place, he couldn't deny his happiness at seeing what was inside the container.

"How much?" he asked as he stepped further into the darkness. The smell of sweat hit him first. He heard muffled cries. Rattling teeth. Shivering. But he distanced himself from it. He had to. After all, this was just business.

"More than enough," Danilo said, leaning against the side of the container door. He puffed on a cigarette, which made Harry want to hurl. Never liked cigarettes, not since they killed his mother.

"You did good. They should shift a fair amount when I get them back to Los Angeles. Sure the trip's gonna be okay?"

Danilo smiled, revealing a mouthful of golden teeth. "Perfect," he said.

Harry took one last look around the container. Looked at the contents inside.

The trip they had planned for this gear wasn't ideal. A trip right through America hauling this container over to Los Angeles. It wasn't easy—it'd take days, and that wasn't including stops. But these beauties went for so much money that it made the trip worthwhile. Besides, since the crackdowns on private travel after the Era of the Ultras, it wasn't like they had a better option. Planes were out of the question. Boats, likewise.

Driving was the only way to do it.

"Ready to talk dollar yet? Danilo asked.

Harry slipped his glasses from his face and wiped his nose. "You know how it works."

"Three times I make this trip. Three times I risk my life, same tiny deposit. I want more. More money. Up front."

Harry was disappointed at Danilo's sudden shift in mood. But he couldn't blame him. In truth, he probably had ripped him off a little. "I'll give you ten thousand up front. But no total pay rise. How's that sound?"

Danilo tilted his head like he was considering. He'd better damn consider it.

"Ten thousand now, five thousand later. Final offer."

Another pause between them. More silence.

Then, Danilo held his hand out to shake Harry's.

It was when Harry grabbed Danilo's hand that he saw the movement in the corner of his eye.

It was over on top of one of the metal containers much like the one the drugs were inside.

At first, Harry thought it must be an animal of some kind. After all, nobody would be around these parts at this time. Everybody knew shit went down at the harbor. Shit you didn't want to risk involving yourself in. You steered clear, stayed away.

So who the hell was this?

"Brad?" Harry had people waiting in the shadows. People watching. He walked over towards the side of the container, the one where he'd seen the movement. It was pitch black down there. He couldn't hear a thing.

He walked a little further down it, holding his breath. It was too quiet. Way too quiet. Usually, he'd hear his goons saying something to one another. Never usually this quiet.

He went to open his mouth when he saw two of his men lying unconscious on the ground.

"What..."

He didn't finish speaking.

A fist smacked his cheek.

He fell back. Hit the ground, slamming the back of his head against the concrete.

The seconds that followed were a blur. He heard Danilo shout something, heard a few shots fired, a grunt of pain.

When he looked up, the taste of blood in his mouth, he saw something impossible. No—something *possible* alright. He'd seen news of the new ULTRA earlier today.

But this wasn't the same one.

This was someone else.

Some *thing* else.

He watched the way the figure in black moved. The way it

jumped around Danilo, taunting him, shifting fluidly from left to right, knocking the gun from his hands, taking him down.

He watched the figure move over to the front of the container—his damned container—and open up the door with total ease.

He saw the figure shoot something inside the container, and his whole world came crashing around him.

He saw the crest of Orion on his chest. Could it be? They said Saint had risen again. Did Saint have a competitor, just like the old times?

He watched his shipment go up in ice. All of it.

And then he watched the man in black turn around. Look over at him. Completely at one with the darkness.

"Too slow," Harry whispered, between a grimace.

He lifted his pistol and fired three times at the figure.

He heard a grunt. Saw a splatter of blood from the figure's side.

Before he could fire and re-aim, he saw the figure run off, disappear into the shadows, limping away.

Harry leaned back and stared up at the moon, a grin on his face. Nycto's competitor. Nycto's competitor! He couldn't stop laughing. Nycto's competitor, and he couldn't even dodge a damn bullet.

If that was Nycto's competitor, then the world was doomed.

If that was Nycto's competitor, then better get on Nycto's side while there was still time.

[28]

You don't know pain until you're shot in the stomach.

I was back home. The sky outside was dark, totally pitch black. The wind rattled against my window as I sat in the complete blackness of my bedroom. I'd turned the TV on just to cover any noise I might make crying out. I had no idea how I'd managed to drag myself back here, get inside, without making any sounds. I'd come all the way from the harbor over on Manhattan Island, and the pain in my stomach, right in the middle, was so sharp that I could barely breathe, let alone speed along with my ULTRA powers.

I lay back on my bed and lifted my clothing. My super black clothing I'd spent so much time perfecting the look of. I could feel dampness through my fingers. So damp that it was making my head spin, making me want to throw up. I knew what the dampness was. I knew what caused dampness like that. Blood. No doubt about it.

I knew I'd been reckless. I'd jumped down into the middle of one of the dodgy dealings at the harbor, which people talked about all the time because I knew it'd bring some attention my way. Some good attention. I wanted to ease people into the idea that more than one ULTRA was back—only not all of them were bad. This one wanted to help people. This one was good. Nycto might've been a sign that things were going to crap, but I wanted to be a sign of hope. A spark of light.

And I'd been shot. I'd been frigging shot.

I lifted my top. When I saw the wound on my stomach, I felt even worse. There was blood coming out of my body. I looked away. I didn't want to look at it. Didn't want to face it. I imagined all the people that were going to find me like this and never knew what I'd been capable of. I imagined Mom coming in during the morning, putting it down to some gang incident or other. Maybe it'd be better if I used the last of my strength to just fly away from here, to disappear forever. At least that way, my parents would live with the smallest hope that I was still alive, out in the world somewhere.

I tried to take a deep breath in, but it hurt too much. I squeezed my eyes shut, felt them sting. Being an ULTRA always looked so easy. The way they used their powers, it was seamless. But now I was finding out for myself that it wasn't as easy as it looked. I'd trained. Hard. But I had a long, long way to go.

If I was going anywhere at all.

And then I remembered something.

The party venue. The doctors said I'd had injuries, but something had happened when I was unconscious. I'd... I'd healed myself in some way.

Maybe it wasn't just a coincidence. Maybe if I focused on this bullet wound, I could heal it, just like I'd woken myself from my coma.

I looked down at my stomach. Tried to focus on the pain it was causing me—wasn't exactly hard. I squeezed my teeth together. *Heal. Heal. Heal.*

But the pain just grew. More blood slipped out. I let out a little babyish yelp.

It was too hard. I didn't have what it took to heal myself, so how the hell was I supposed to make people believe in me?

I was about to close my eyes when I saw what was flickering on the television screen in the corner of my bedroom.

It was a breaking news scene from the harbor over on Manhattan Island. Something happened. My head was so light that I could barely make out the words.

And then they clicked: MYSTERY MAN CAUSES CHAOS AT HARBOR: ULTRA?

I felt a twinge of pride inside. A speck of joy. They were at the scene of the crime. The police were apprehending the suspects. And...

Oh no.

Oh God no.

The next shot showed that container that I'd destroyed the drugs in. Only there were a lot of stunned people standing around it. A lot of police, armed, and grainy footage of a man firing at some civilians as they ran away.

Most of them got away. Most of them fled.

But one of them fell.

"Obviously, this just shows what happens when an ULTRA tries to police the world," the police officer said. "We had this here under control. Now... now it's all fallen apart. We've got a young lady dead. And that's all because of the ULTRAs trying to go about business in their own way, just like they did the last time they were around."

I felt a twinge of responsibility as I saw that footage replay of the poor fleeing woman hit the road and go still. I'd started this chaos. I'd wanted to help, but I'd caused a death in the process. I was responsible for the death of an innocent person.

As my head grew lighter, I started to wonder if maybe it

would be better if I just faded to sleep. Maybe it would be better if I just...

I heard the floor to the left of my bed creak.

I felt a breeze touch my skin.

Funny story. Ever since I'd been a little kid, I'd sworn this bedroom was haunted. The sound of the floor on my left creaking—which it only ever did when someone stood on it. Always followed by a breeze from a window that I swore I'd shut. Always.

But never had I seen anyone standing over me. Never.

I turned over to look anyway. To check that the ghost who obviously wouldn't be there *wasn't* there.

When I saw the figure standing over me as I lay in my bed, I wasn't sure how to react.

A man in a black trench coat. He was wearing Doc Marten boots, a plain mask over his face. And on his head, a bowler hat.

I tried to scream.

But all the strength slipped from my body as the pain from the wound took a hold.

I wanted to fight. I wanted to get away. But the wound. It was so strong...

"You're not getting off that bed with a wound like that."

The voice made me go even colder than I already was. I looked around. I swore I'd heard the voice right in front, over in the shadows. But I couldn't see anyone or anything there.

I felt my heart pick up. Pressure built up in my head. I needed to act fast. Needed to get away.

I focused on that bullet wound in my stomach. And as painful as it was, I put all my fear and discomfort flow into that patch of skin on my torso. I let the deepest, darkest memories come back. Memories I didn't even know I had—memories of being dunked under water when I was just a baby. Memories of echoing voices. Of someone standing over me. Of muffled words that I couldn't place, that I didn't understand. Memories from dreams that seemed weirdly real. I didn't know where they were from. I didn't know where they'd come from.

I just knew that the memories were painful ones.

And then I realized my stomach wasn't hurting as much anymore.

I opened my eyes and couldn't believe what I was looking at.

The wound on my stomach was gone. Completely gone. No scars, nothing like that. Like it'd... like it'd healed over.

I saw movement to my left, snapping me right back into the moment.

"You did well," the Man in the Bowler Hat said, his voice incredibly deep. "To heal your wound. You've got strength. But you need to stop being stupid if you want to get anywhere."

I didn't know what to say. I couldn't believe this man was actually addressing *me*. Like he knew what my powers were. What I was capable of. "I don't—I don't know what you're—"

"Don't try the naivety game with me," the Man in the Bowler Hat said. "I know what you are. What you can do. I know what you're capable of. I've seen it, Kyle Peters. I've seen what you are."

My stomach almost dropped out of my body. He knew who I was. He knew who the hell I was.

"How—how do you—"

"For one, you've not got your costume on right now. And you look awfully similar to that spotty little nerd I saw on the school photographs in your living room. So I'd say that's a giveaway."

I felt myself blush. "But how do you know who... *who* I am?"

"It doesn't take a genius to figure out who you were," he said. "And that should be a serious worry for you. Because now Nycto is rising, the government aren't going to go easy on you.

They're going to want you just as much as they want him. And as much as you want to go on living your nice little double life, it's dangerous, Kyle. You need to let Kyle die. You need to become somebody else entirely."

The Man in the Bowler Hat turned around. Started to walk away from me. I still couldn't believe what was happening here, in the comfort of my bedroom. It all seemed so surreal.

"You're strong physically," the Man in the Bowler Hat said. "But mentally, you are weak."

"I'd watch what you say," I said, in the pussiest voice imaginable.

The Man in the Bowler Hat stopped. Turned around. "Your mental weaknesses are the only thing holding you back, even if you're afraid to admit that right now. If you can believe yourself, truly believe in yourself, you can achieve the one thing you've been gifted these abilities for."

"And what's that?" I asked even though I was already afraid I knew the answer.

"You know exactly what it is. You know exactly what you have to do. You have to stop Nycto. You're the only person who can."

The Man in the Bowler Hat walked further away. There were so many things I wanted to ask him, so many questions I had. "What if I can't?"

The Man in the Bowler Hat stopped again. "If you can't, then God help us all."

I looked down at myself. My skinny body. I was just Kyle Peters. When I wasn't in my costume, that's all I was.

But I knew this person, whoever it was, had a point.

Even when I was in my costume, I was still being Kyle Peters. I was still being myself.

I had to change. I had to fight. If I wanted to defeat Nycto, I had to adapt.

I lifted my head to ask the Man in the Bowler Hat who he was, how I could find him. He seemed like the mentor I needed right now, even though I was clueless about his morals, his motives.

But when I lifted my head to ask the questions, the Man in the Bowler Hat had disappeared.

29

I lay back across my bed and thought about what the Man in the Bowler Hat told me.

If it had even happened at all. I was growing more and more convinced that the encounter was the product of blood loss. That I'd dreamed it all.

Still, it resonated with me.

It was a bright summer day. The air was warm, and I knew that Central Park would usually be full of happy people on a day like today. People way cooler than me, sure, people I was infinitely jealous of, absolutely, but people nonetheless.

But as news of Nycto's attacks became more common, more terrifying, and even scarier than anything, more *random* in their nature, I knew Central Park wouldn't be a place where many people would be all that interested in spending time today.

I listened to the silence of my street, outside my house. It was a Monday, but we'd been given a few days off school after the events at the party venue, as well as because of Nycto's attacks. We were finishing for summer at the end of the week anyway, so everything had a kind of anti-climactic feel to it. In truth, I knew we'd probably never go back to school this year. Most people would just take the rest of the week off.

What a way to mark the end of another year. Never the way I'd expected it to go down.

The more I heard and the more I read about Nycto's destruction, the more those words from the Man in the Bowler Hat resonated with me. He'd told me I needed to do something. That I was the only person that *could* do something.

Nycto had launched a fresh attack on London earlier today. Moments later, just as the UK government was getting over the attack, he launched another attack back home in Austin. Then another over in Zanzibar City, attacking a ferry terminal. Then another, back home in Boston, just up the highway. The world was reeling from the first few attacks. No one had any idea where he was going to strike next.

But the truth was clear: he was getting through cities and places around the world, and he wasn't letting anyone or anything get in his way.

I focused on the locations of the attacks, knowing I couldn't just let more people die and suffer. I was an ULTRA, for better or for worse. I had to use that to my full advantage. The Man in the Bowler Hat said it himself—I was the only one capable of stopping Nycto. I just had to believe in myself. Shake off my mental weakness, or whatever he called it.

I closed my eyes and pictured the scenes of Nycto's attacks in my mind.

As the memories of the party attack and the loss that came with it flooded my mind, I felt myself thinking quicker. Trying to connect dots between Nycto's attacks at super-speed. There was a pattern. There had to be a pattern somewhere. Sure, the attacks *looked* random, but nothing was ever truly random. There was always a logic. Always a—

I heard a knock on the door downstairs. It snapped me out

of my thoughts in an instant.

My parents were out shopping, so I climbed off the bed and staggered down the stairs. I wasn't sure who it could be. And as I lowered the handle, I got a little worried after what the Man in the Bowler Hat told me he'd easily tracked me down.

My worry soon slipped away when I saw Ellicia standing at the door.

Her dark hair shone in the sunlight. She smiled at me, revealing that little gap between her teeth. "Hello, stranger," she said. "You okay?"

I couldn't find the right words to say to Ellicia. I mean, she was here, at my damned door. What the hell was I supposed to say?

I took a deep breath. Decided to play it as cool as I could. "Hey."

Ellicia looked around me, over my shoulder. "You up to much?"

"Oh, er, homework. Just homework. You?"

I blushed, realizing my mistake right away. We didn't have any homework. How stupid could I be?

Ellicia shrugged. "Just wondered if you... Just passing by. Thought I'd say hello."

She smiled at me. I saw her eyes light up in that way that always made me light up inside too. But what did I say now?

I wanted to invite her in. Ask her to come into my house. But I heard the Man in the Bowler Hat's voice in my head.

"You need to let Kyle die. You need to become somebody else entirely."

I didn't want to believe him. But the thought of anything else happening to Ellicia all because I was failing to take on Nycto... it wasn't worth thinking about.

"If you're busy," Ellicia said, drawing that last word out. "Maybe another time."

I should've said no. I should've said I wasn't busy. I was a sixteen-year-old kid—*this* was the life I was supposed to be living.

"Yeah," I said, scratching my head. "I'll Facebook you. Or somethin'."

Ellicia lowered her head. Smiled and nodded. "Right. Facebook."

She turned around and started to walk away. I hadn't felt this much an idiot in a long time.

"My boyfriend's left me," Ellicia said.

Talk about not knowing what to say. How the hell was I supposed to say a thing to this?

"Oh," I said. "That's... that's too bad."

She nodded. "Moved over to Chicago. His parents don't think New York's safe anymore. Not with Nycto. Not after everything that's happened."

I started to say something back to Ellicia when it clicked.

A sudden realization clicked in my mind.

Austin.

Zanzibar City.

Boston.

Yaizu.

An alphabet of American cities. A reverse alphabet of foreign cities.

C was coming next.

The biggest populated American city beginning with C?

Chicago. Chicago.

"I'll see you soon," I said to Ellicia, fully aware of how much of an idiot I sounded now.

She smiled at me, and it pained me to close the door on her.

But I ran upstairs.

Changed rapidly into my gear, faster than I thought was capable.

I looked in the mirror at myself. Looked at myself, the costume split from where the bullet hit me. The only thing not on was the black hood.

"You're not causing any more chaos, Nycto," I whispered to myself. "Not anymore."

I pulled the black mask on.

Then, I shot out of my house.

I'd never been to Chicago before. I figured now was as good a time as any to take a trip.

NYCTO FLOATED at the corner of Sherman Avenue.

He'd suspected Kyle Peters for so long. So, so long. Right since he first saw footage of that hooded assailant helping the woman at the ATM. He thought he recognized his scrawny figure, that goofy way he ran. But he hadn't really believed it. Not totally. There hadn't been enough to go on.

He hadn't believed Kyle Peters was capable of the things *he* was capable of.

Not until he saw him shoot out of his house, thinking he was completely camouflaged.

Well, nothing was camouflaged to Nycto. Nycto saw things exactly as they were.

He thought about going into Kyle's house. To putting a stop to his nonsense before he got the chance.

But he could tell from Kyle's excitement that he was falling right into his trap. He'd seen the clues, and he was stumbling into them like the little idiot he'd always been.

He watched the dark-haired girl, Ellicia, walk away from Kyle's house. He'd deal with her if he had to. In time, he'd deal with her.

But now it was time for Nycto to have some fun.

It was time to head to Chicago.

30

My first visit to Chicago wasn't exactly under the best circumstances.

It was cooler here than it was back in New York, living up to the stereotype of the Windy City. The sun covered with cloud. Otherwise, it was pretty reminiscent of Manhattan in all truth. The same tall buildings, the same honking horns of taxis. The same sense that usually, this was a city that was busy. That was bustling with life.

But today, there was a strange quietness to it. A quietness that I knew would be the same in every city around the world.

People weren't venturing far from home when Nycto was such a threat.

I sat on a bench overlooking North Avenue beach. The waves were high, and apparently this place usually got pretty busy. There were just a few people out today, sitting and hoping for sun. Behind me, the horns of cars, the chatter of the city.

I had my gear on underneath a big black coat I was wearing. I also had sunglasses on, which probably should've made me look cool but actually made me look stupid. I did what the shifty older generation always did when they were trying not to look suspicious—held up a newspaper. I mean, man. Holding an actual paper version of the news in this year? How the hell was that supposed to *not* look suspicious?

The only thing that mattered was that there was no sign of Nycto yet.

I overheard chatter about the ULTRAs, mostly Nycto. A few worried conversations in cafes, mostly empty. But the talk wasn't all about Nycto. There was talk about the incident in New York, too. The rumors of another ULTRA causing a scene at the harbor, but causing chaos in the process. Me, of course. They didn't know that yet. I was kinda glad. Some people didn't exactly have the nicest things to say about ULTRAs in general, even when we were just trying to do the right thing.

I heard some shouts over to my left. Saw people walking through the streets. They were holding placards in the air, chanting things.

"Go away, ULTRAS!"

"BURN IN HELL!"

"Je Suis Humanity!"

I saw those placards, heard the angry chants, and I felt uneasy about this whole thing. I'd made an educated guess that Nycto had Chicago next on his list if there really was a pattern to how he was going about his attacks. But what if I was wrong? What if *I'd* made an error, and he was hovering above another city right now, waiting to rain down those fireballs from his fists?

I shuffled my newspaper. There wasn't much worrying about it could do. I was here, where I thought Nycto was headed. That was the main thing.

I hadn't thought nearly enough about what my plan would be when Nycto finally got here. Part of me wanted to reach out to him. To figure out who he was. Ask who he was and why exactly he was doing what he was doing, masks off. Everyone had a reason for the things they did. Maybe I could get through to Nycto. Maybe I could reach some place inside him that he didn't even know was there, turn him around before he caused any chaos.

I sat on that park bench for ages. After a while, at least an hour, I walked into an alleyway and camouflaged. I used every inch of strength in my body to hover up between the buildings. I was ropey at it. Nearly fell a few times. The height made me feel sick.

But I managed to lift myself right above the city, my fear of heights—something I didn't even know I had until now—well and truly awakening.

The city was still. There was no sign of Nycto. No...

I saw it. Saw it in the corner of my eye.

Movement. Up ahead to the right.

Nycto.

I felt myself grow more at ease hovering in the sky right then. Like the fury of seeing Nycto fueled my powers.

I felt the sickness in my stomach. The nervousness telling me I was being crazy. That this was suicide.

I had no choice. I was the only person capable of stopping Nycto. And I wasn't even hundred percent sure I was that.

I flew in Nycto's direction. As I shot through the sky, my stomach tickling with adrenaline and fear, I felt myself flying faster towards him.

He shot to the left. Then to the right. He was moving crazy fast. So fast that I had no idea if I'd actually be able to catch him.

Then, something weird happened. He stopped. He stopped and he started dropping. Dropping in free-fall out of the sky.

I hesitated for a moment. It seemed weird. Like something wasn't right. Why was he falling? Had his powers failed him?

Screw it. If they had, this was my moment.

I flew down towards Nycto. As I got closer, I became more suspicious. More unsure. But I had to get him. I had to stop him.

I was just inches away from him. I could almost feel his silver armor. I could see that metal...

Wait.

This wasn't the same mask Nycto wore.

This wasn't...

I collided with what I thought was Nycto.

My image of him blurred. The Nycto I'd seen disappeared.

I was holding on to something else entirely.

Something big. Something... something metal.

A bomb.

I looked up. Saw the real Nycto hovering over me. And I wanted to turn around. I wanted to turn around and go after him.

But I needed to stop this bomb.

I could see people below. Terrified people fleeing. A woman with a pram, startled; another kid beside her holding an ice cream and staring up with fear in her eyes.

I gripped on tight to the bomb.

Gripped on tight and felt myself get stronger.

The bomb was just feet from the ground now.

"If you can believe yourself, truly believe in yourself, you can achieve the one thing you've been gifted these abilities for."

I had to stop it. I had to use all my strength. I had to...

The bomb came within inches of the ground.

I flipped underneath it.

Pushed it over towards one of the buildings on my right, one of the skyscrapers, with everything I had.

I slammed into the ground, a crater forming around me. I heard voices. Heard screams.

All I could do was watch that bomb that'd left my hands. The bomb I'd stopped hitting the ground of Chicago.

Watch it fly towards the massive skyscraper as if it was in slow motion.

I wanted to get up. I wanted to stop it. I knew if I pulled myself out of this smoky pit, my back wrecking with pain, that I'd have the power and the force to stop it.

But then I saw the bomb hit the side of the building.

I saw the light flash. Saw the glass splinter out of the building as the explosion ripped through Chicago, the skyscraper tumbling to one side.

And then I saw Nycto floating above. Watching. He was far away, but I swore he was smiling.

I bit my lip through the pain in my back and shifted it as well as I could. I climbed out of the crater with shaky hands as smoke billowed from the falling skyscraper, as sirens instantaneously erupted around Chicago.

When I climbed out of that pit onto my shaky legs, I wasn't met with the friendly faces of people pleased to be saved.

I saw the fear. Saw the horror. People looked at me and screamed. Some of them threw things at me. Spat at me.

"It's one of them!" a woman cried.

"Monster! Another monster!"

I stood there and watched the top half of the skyscraper crumble towards the streets below, raining down glass and debris.

And I knew what had happened. I knew what Nycto had done.

He'd made me look the villain.

He'd lured me in, and he'd made me throw that bomb into the building.

Now, I was just an enemy. Just a monster. Just like him.

Except I was broken and bruised.

And armed police were hurtling in my direction.

31

I'd be lying if I said I'd ever been popular.

But being chased by armed police units dispatched by the United States government and framed for the destruction of one of Chicago's largest buildings?

Yeah. I reckon my popularity had just about hit rock bottom.

I sprinted away from the oncoming armed police. Everything blurred around me—buildings, people. I could hear shouts and cries; helicopters above. The air was ripe with the smell of burning, a smell I'd grown too used to recently. I felt sick. Felt like throwing up, as every inch of my body ached with pain. No matter how much I pushed myself, I didn't feel like I could move to my full potential after the spine-crushing fall through the earth just moments ago. Whenever I tried that teleportation trick I *knew* I was capable of, it just didn't work.

I was weak compared to Nycto. I saw that clearly now. Now more than ever. He was so much stronger than me. Not just that, but he'd framed me. He was trying to drag me down to his level.

All I could do right now? Run like I was the villain everyone made me out to be.

I saw some police cars up ahead. Saw Chicago PD pointing their guns at me. I didn't want to brush them out of the way. Doing that would only further prove Nycto's framing of me. I didn't want to hurt anyone. I knew I'd be national news already. The logo on my chest of Orion's stars. I imagined the fear of people around the world. And the fear of people I knew. Mom. Dad. Damon. Ellicia.

If they knew the truth, I wondered how much they'd hate me.

I heard the gunshots fire from the police up ahead.

I vaulted up in the air. Wasn't easy, but it was the best I could manage right now.

I ran up into the air like I was climbing steps. Awkward, wobbly steps, but steps nonetheless. I didn't want to take another bullet. Sure, I could heal myself, but healing took too much focus, too much effort. Best thing for me to do right now was to get the hell out of Chicago. Get myself away from the scene and out of the frame before anyone could place me here in any way.

I remembered what the Man in the Bowler Hat told me as I somersaulted into the air, dodging the police bullets. He'd told me that it wasn't hard for him to find me, Kyle Peters. So if he found me, others would. I'd been stupid coming here. I'd fallen right into Nycto's trap.

I shot down a street. I needed to fly back to New York. I could try teleporting but felt too surrounded, too watched. Besides, I wasn't feeling confident about the teleportation. It seemed to sap my energy more than anything. I'd tried tele-porting here in the first place, but it'd taken too much out of me so I'd decided to just fly my way over at super-speed. An experi-ence that I closed my eyes for the most of, sure.

I heard more sirens. Saw news teams gathering around the fallen mass of the building I'd destroyed. I'd done it 'cause I was trying to protect that woman and her children. I was trying to help people on the streets of Chicago.

And now I was being hunted.

I saw more police up ahead. When I turned around, more were heading my way. I was cornered. Surrounded.

"Stop right there!" a voice shouted. Then more voices followed through the loudspeakers, all of them barking commands at me like I was some kind of terrorist, urging me to stand down as if I actually intended to hurt anyone here.

I wanted to fight my case. Tell everyone in this city I wasn't with Nycto. That this was a mistake. That I'd been set up, and that I was just a kid who wanted to help; the only kid who could help. But did I really believe that still? Did I honestly think I could take down Nycto when he was so obviously way more powerful than me? I wasn't sure.

I saw the police cars approaching. I wanted to help. I didn't want to run away like I was guilty.

But what choice did I have?

I shot up into the sky. As I rose, I felt the bullets whoosh past me. I kept on going, heading right towards the clouds, the height making me feel sickly all over again.

When I was high enough, I looked down at the city below. I saw the smoke. The flames. I could feel the frustration in the streets. I could sense them looking up at me, everyone; like I was another monster here to bring their world to an end.

I'd caused this. Whether I'd meant to or not, whether I wanted to face up to it or not, I'd caused this.

And I'd have to make up for it.

I focused on all that pain and I felt myself shifting away from here. I felt that tingling in my scalp that I always got when I mastered the teleportation. I thought about the loss. The pain. The anger. And I felt myself getting further and further back home. I practically saw the outline of my bedroom right in front of me.

And then something hit me.

Something smacked into my right.

Knocked me out of my trance.

I felt a bang. An explosion ripped through my side, made my head feel like it was going to burst.

Instinctively, I closed my eyes. Listened to the ringing in my ears. Tasted metal in my mouth.

When I opened my eyes again, I couldn't believe what was in front of me.

I wasn't in Chicago anymore. I was... well, I didn't know where I was. Just that I was at the top of a mountain somewhere. Somewhere right in the middle of the ocean.

No, wait. Not at the top of a mountain. At the top of a volcano.

Smoke billowed out from the volcano. I could feel the heat from it. I stood up, stretched out my snapped arm, healing it in a painful few moments. I walked closer to the volcano, no idea how I'd ended up here. Had something gone wrong with the teleportation? Had I screwed it up, proven my rustiness, once again?

When I saw who was on the opposite side of the volcano mouth, I knew right away that my suspicions were wrong.

"Hello, friend," Nycto said, hovering above the ground. "I think it's about time we had a chat, don't you?"

32

"Well? All this way and you've got nothing to say to me?"

I stared across the mouth of the volcano at Nycto. The light was dark blue like the early hours, as if sunrise was on its way, which seemed strange because it'd only been the middle of the afternoon when I was back in Chicago. Explained just how far from home I was. All around me, vast openness as I stood atop this volcano. All around me, silence. The smell of sulfur piercing the air, bitter and tangy. Loneliness. Totally loneliness.

Except for Nycto.

"I didn't want to have to do all the talking," he said. There was a light shining from him which revealed our surroundings, made the sea feel even vaster all around us. "But it's looking like I'm gonna have to."

I couldn't quite believe I was facing up against Nycto. It seemed surreal. I mean, I'd seen what he was capable of on the television, all over the internet. I'd heard the fear he struck in people. He was an ULTRA, for heaven's sakes, the first one I'd truly come face to face with. The Man in the Bowler Hat didn't exactly count. And he was hardly doing much to help me right now.

Even though I was technically an ULTRA too, it felt like I was playing the part. Like I was just in costume for Halloween.

But Nycto...

Nycto was the real deal.

And that was terrifying.

"Krakatoa's a place I've always wanted to visit," Nycto said. He hovered down and perched on the edge of the volcano. He was wearing that silver armor—the same armor the guy who destroyed my party venue had worn. "In 1883, this rock exploded. Wiped over thirty-thousand people off the face of the earth. One of the most brutal natural disasters in history." He sounded like he was enjoying speaking about the eruption a little too much. "Always found places like this fascinating. Just, you know. Couldn't grow the balls to actually face my fears and see the world outside my home."

"You've done more than that," I muttered under my breath, not sure whether cockiness with a monster like Nycto was such a good idea.

But Nycto laughed. His voice was deep and inhuman, but he sounded like he had a sense of humor. Like a regular human being. "I knew you'd confront me eventually. You always were a moral one, even though you were terrified of everything. Heart in the right place."

I listened to Nycto's words and they made the hairs on my arms stand up. Nycto knew me? How... how did he know who I was?

"It's over," I said, trying to sound as strong as I could. "The chaos. The destruction. All of it. It's over."

Nycto laughed again. He nodded. Looked down into the mouth of the volcano. I could see smoke billowing up out of it. The air I was breathing grew warmer, ash starting to rain down.

"I could make this explode with the click of my fingers," he said. "But the pair of us... Well, we're strong enough that we wouldn't even *have* to click our fingers."

"What're you trying to say?" I said.

Nycto stood again. He stepped over the mouth of the volcano. Stood over it, so assured on the thin air. "Your talk of fighting. The reason we're here. Tell me, what is it for? What is any of it for?"

"What is stopping you killing people for? What is stopping you destroying cities for? Are you seriously asking me that question?"

"People are overrated," Nycto said. I sensed the air getting thicker. I wasn't sure whether it was because I was getting angrier or Nycto was getting gradually more impatient. I figured it was probably a combination of the two. "The ULTRAs were put on this planet for a reason in the first place. People had their time. The ULTRAs were supposed to have their time."

"I don't know how you can say that. The ULTRAs were created to *protect* humanity. Not destroy it."

Nycto tilted his head to one side as if there wasn't much of a difference between the two. "Maybe originally. Maybe that's how it was supposed to play out. Or maybe God made it look that way. Maybe God put the ULTRAs on Earth to wipe the slate clean. To end the virus of people. Because that's what humanity is. Don't you see? All the war, all the abuse of power. They are problems created by humans. And they are problems we can end. Together."

I was speechless. I heard what Nycto was saying. Sure, people could be pretty shitty. I'd spent my whole life thinking as much. But this?

"You talk about power abuse," I said. "How are you any different when you're going round attacking those weaker than you?"

"Does a lion feel guilty when it hunts down the gazelle? Of course not. It's the food chain. It's the way the world works. The balance of all things. Does an antidote feel guilty for attacking the flu? No. So why should we feel guilty for wiping the scourge of humanity from existence?"

I quickly realized that Nycto wasn't going to be bargainable with. He was mad. Completely and utterly mad.

"We can rule this place," Nycto said. He lifted his hands. "Look all around you. Look at this pure, natural beauty. This could be our playground. The start of a new era free of humanity's destruction. Listen to the birds. Listen to the wind. Listen to the—"

"I *would* listen, if a raging psychopath wasn't spouting shit at the top of his voice," I said.

Nycto laughed again like he genuinely found my words amusing. "I know what you're like. I know you'll come round to the temptation soon enough."

"You don't know a thing about me," I said, tightening my fist.

"That's not exactly true. Kyle."

When Nycto dropped to the ground, I felt as if my whole world was collapsing around me.

He'd said my name. He knew who I was. He knew exactly who I was.

But that wasn't even the thing that startled me most.

The thing that startled me most was when Nycto lifted his mask.

Dropped it to the ground.

It took a few seconds for the person I was looking at to truly register. I grew more and more convinced that this was some kind of weird dream. Some kind of nightmare.

But no. It was real.

The person in front of me was Daniel Septer.

"Daniel?" I said.

Daniel smiled at me. He looked so much bulkier than the skinny, lanky kid with greasy hair I'd known him as from a grade below me at school. Daniel made me look cool, let's put it that way. He was a weakling. A wuss of the highest order. If I was at the bottom of the food chain, Daniel was swimming under the chain in the sewerage waters below.

But no. He wasn't anymore.

Daniel was Nycto.

"How... how..."

"I know," Daniel said, floating with such swagger, such confidence. "Changed a bit, hmm?"

"You were—"

"Off sick? Sure. I was sick. Sick of people. Sick of the bullies. Sick of the way everyone's treated me and my family my entire life."

I shook my head. It wasn't the only part of my body shaking. "Daniel you..." Seeing it was Daniel humanized Nycto. It made me feel like I *could* help him. Sway him. Turn him around. "You can't do this. You don't want to do this. Surely this isn't what you want."

"But it *is* what I want," Daniel said, the smile clear on his face. "And I know, deep down, it's what you want too. Because we aren't so different, me and you. We've both been screwed over by the vermin at school."

"You killed people. From our school."

Daniel shrugged. "They woulda done it to me if they'd kept on the way they were going."

"You killed... you killed Mike Beacon."

"Mike Beacon?" Daniel's face looked startled. "Why in hell's name would I give a shit about that jock? And why would you?"

I felt my anger reach a bursting point then with the memory

of storming into that party venue and finding Damon and Ellicia on the floor. Pulling them out of the mouth of certain death. "You're a scumbag. You're no better than the people who bullied you. You're worse."

Daniel smiled. He lifted his Nycto helmet again. It hovered beside his face. "I've learned to embrace the hate so much, Kyle. I could teach you everything I know. We could teach each other. We could end all this madness right now. It's really quite fun when you get into it. Seeing their faces when they know it's about to..."

I couldn't listen to Daniel's bullshit any longer.

I threw myself through the air. Hurtled right towards his chest, across the mouth of the volcano. I'd throw him in there. Plunge him into the lava.

"Never!" I shouted, as loud as I could. "Never!"

I felt the impact impending.

And then I stopped.

I stopped, right in the middle of the air, like I'd hit a glass wall.

"Might want to look down before you make any rash decisions, Kyle," Daniel said. The Nycto mask covered his face. He was back to his horrifying alter-ego again. "You know where I am when you need me. If I haven't changed my mind on you, that is." His voice was deep again. Menacing.

I tried to shake free, get past the invisible wall, wrap my hands around Nycto's neck.

But when I looked down into the mouth of the volcano, I forgot about Nycto. I forgot about Daniel. I forgot about everything.

My parents were lying next to one another thirty feet below me. Hovering over the volcano, over the lava pit, just like I was.

"Be careful," Nycto said, floating further away. "I know who you are. And if you try anything, *anything*, I'll put everyone you ever cared about through the worst pain imaginable."

I felt tears building in my eyes at the sight of my mom's terrified face. At the confusion on my dad's.

"I'll see you again sometime," Nycto said. He pulled his hands apart. "Oh. Enjoy the ride."

He slammed his hands together and disappeared in a flash of light.

The second he disappeared, so too did the wall in front of me.

The second he disappeared, my parents fell down toward the lava.

33

I watched my parents fall down into the belly of the volcano and I didn't even think.

I threw myself in their direction. Dodged the rocks falling all around me from the mouth. I didn't hear anything. I didn't even notice the intensifying stench of sulfur.

The only thing that mattered to me were my parents, and making sure I saved them.

I watched the walls of the volcano close in. It grew darker, Nycto's light above now gone, so I squeezed my eyes and found myself beaming a light down toward them. I could see the look of fear on their faces. The look of terror.

They were hurtling to their deaths. Nycto had sent them hurtling to their deaths. He knew who I was, and even after his massive speech to try and win me over to his way of thinking, he still had my parents as leverage.

What kind of a bastard was he after all?

I saw the orange glow of the lava right below me. As fast as I flew, my parents seemed to be falling faster. I was pushing myself. Pushing myself to my absolute max. But it wasn't enough. They were falling. They were going to hit the lava unless I did something; unless I acted.

I gritted my teeth into my lips and thought of all the misery my parents had been through, how different it would've been if Cassie was still here. Because her death was the reason. Her death was the reason for everything bad they felt.

Maybe if I'd been quicker when I was a kid, I could've saved her.

Maybe I wouldn't have failed them after all.

I saw them disappearing further away. Saw them on the verge of being swallowed by the lava. I knew they were probably gone already. People didn't just survive falls like this. The toxic in the air, it'd probably killed them.

But I wasn't giving up on them. I wasn't letting them die. Nycto might've sent a message loud and clear, but that didn't matter right now. All that mattered were my parents.

I tried to stop them midair using my telekinesis, or whatever it was. But it was too hard. I could only use one power or the other, and right now my focus was on flying toward them. I was too weak to use two of my stronger powers at once. I needed to keep on pushing. Fast.

I saw them just meters above the lava and I knew it was over.

I felt pain inside. A sharper pain than I'd ever felt, as rocks fell down from above me. I could feel the heat from the lava burning my face, the sulfur in the air choking me.

I'd failed them. I'd let them die. I'd missed my chance to act against Nycto, to get to his level of strength, and he'd punished me for it.

He was stronger than me. There was no doubt about that now.

All I had left to do was try.

I felt power building within, right in the middle of my chest.

I didn't understand it, only that it was swelling, getting stronger, more intense.

I could feel the power moving into my hands. An electricity. Ultimate anger... no. Not anger. *Love.* Love for my parents. Love for who they were. For everything they'd done for me.

They tumbled towards the lava.

I lifted my hands. It felt like there was something between them, like a magnetic force.

I remembered what Nycto did. How he'd clapped his hands together just moments ago, caused this crazy race down the volcano to start.

I had to do what he did. I knew there was no other way now.

I slammed my hands together.

They bolted apart, again like magnets rejecting each other.

Only I saw something shooting out from my palms.

It was ice. Pure ice, flowing like water. I could feel it freezing my hands. Making my body shake all over.

It fired out of my hands and hurtled towards the bottom of the volcano. I didn't know how it was happening. I didn't know how a thing like this could be possible—I mean, it *wasn't* possible, not within the realms of humanity. I wasn't sure I'd even seen another ULTRA do something like this in all the old video clips, the YouTube uploads.

But it was happening.

I watched the ice hit the lava. And right away, as more of that blue ice-like substance hit the lava, I saw the lava's rumbling, which I assumed Daniel had started, ease. I saw its color change from orange to a dulled pink, then to a gray, then... blue, just like the stuff that'd come out of my hands.

But my parents were still falling towards it.

I moved my focus. Pointed the ice at them. Not directly at them, but at their arms.

I grabbed them. Grabbed them and eased their falls with the

ice, then gently dropped them down on the frozen lava. I heard it crack, start to split. I didn't have long. I had to get them out of here.

I flew down and landed on the ice beside them. They held on to one another, Dad's eyes wide, Mom gasping with fear.

I wanted to hug them like I was their son. I wanted to tell them they were okay. That I was here.

But I couldn't be their son. Not right now. I had to get them home first.

I walked over to them. Grabbed both of their shoulders. The power within me that my love for them had awakened made me feel stronger than ever before; more powerful than ever before.

Dad looked up at me, puzzlement and fear in his eyes. "Where... where are..."

I focused all my attention, all my power, on getting back home.

I heard a crack split through my head.

When the crack ended, I was back home. My parents were beside me.

Dad was silent. So too was Mom. We were in their bedroom, in the peace and quiet, away from the madness of the volcano. It was still light, a contrast to the pitch blackness of Indonesia.

They looked at each other. Didn't look at me, just each other.

And then they fell back on the bed and passed out.

I tucked them in. I wasn't sure how long they'd be out. They'd be in shock, and I had to keep a close eye on them.

I went back to my room. Pulled off my hood. Took off the rest of my gear and threw it onto the floor. I perched on the edge of my bed, my heart racing, my head spinning.

I didn't want this. I didn't want to be an ULTRA. I didn't *want* this responsibility. Sure, Daniel Septer might've been weak how I used to know him. But he was Nycto now, and Nycto was strong. Too strong.

I couldn't compete.

I couldn't fight.

I just wanted to be Kyle again.

I tucked my head in my arms.

I cried.

I DIDN'T SEE IT, but on the television, the news showed images of the destruction in Chicago; of me, in my outfit.

The greatest threat to humanity, they were calling me, calling Nycto. A shortcut to near-certain extinction. An enemy of humanity.

They were coming for me.

And I couldn't fight it anymore.

I just couldn't fight.

34

I stared down into the mouth of the same volcano I'd rescued my parents from just hours ago.

I wasn't dressed in my gear. I knew it was dangerous, but it was just how it had to be right now. For me to do what I had to do. Finish my job.

I could see the lava right at the bottom of the volcano again. Whatever I'd done to it, whatever my cursed powers had made happen, they'd been undone. Which was just as well. It's what I'd been hoping for.

The sky was lighter now. Sunrise was approaching. There was total peace around this place. It'd been hard work forcing my way here. It'd taken hours in itself to activate the teleportation I knew I was capable of. I'd ended up in rubble; I'd ended up in the middle of streets. I was rusty. So rusty, especially compared to Nycto. So weak.

That's just who I was. That's just who I'd always been.

And that was why I couldn't save anyone.

I smelled the sulfur below, and it brought back the memories of the fight to save my parents' lives earlier. The silence now contrasted the chaos earlier; the chaos that started with Nycto—

Daniel Septer—revealing who he was, revealing he knew who I was.

I wanted to fight. I really did. I wanted to use what I had for good. To make sure no more people around the world had to suffer at the hands of this psychopath.

But I didn't have it in me. I didn't have the strength. I didn't have the power. I didn't have anything.

I lifted the suit I'd spent so long carefully choosing. A suit I felt proud of when I'd first seen myself in it, stared at myself in the mirror wearing it. Stupid, really. Because the Man in the Bowler Hat was wrong. No matter what I covered myself in, I was always going to be Kyle Peters underneath. I was always going to be the same loser. Daniel Septer might've been able to shake his loser image, but look how that'd turned out for him. He was the enemy. The enemy I was trying to fight. Trying to stop.

The enemy I'd failed to stop.

I felt a lump swell in my throat as I held that suit further over the smoky open mouth of the volcano. A voice in my head told me not to do this. Not to give up. To keep on working. To keep on fighting. To believe in myself.

But I couldn't.

How could I believe in myself especially now my parents and God knows who else were at risk?

How could I believe in myself when Daniel Septer—the guy destroying the planet—knew exactly who I was, *what* I was?

There was only one thing to do. Only one way out.

I held my breath.

I dropped my suit down into the mouth of the volcano.

I watched it fall. Watched the identity I so wanted to be descend into the lava.

When it drifted out of sight, I teleported myself back home.

I was never using my powers again.

35

Three weeks later...

ANOTHER DAY, another city randomly terrorized by Nycto.

I sat on my bed and watched the news enrolling on the television in front of me. My eyes stung, and the headlines kinda mashed together, I'd been staring at the screen that long. I felt like if I sat here any longer, I simply wouldn't exist.

But what else was I supposed to do? What was anyone supposed to do?

The sun was beaming outside my bedroom window. We were two weeks into the summer break now, although it was a different kind of break, that was for sure. Summer was a scorcher, and despite all the panic over Nycto's random attacks, which had claimed casualties in over twenty global cities over the last three weeks, there were the sounds of laughter out on the streets. The sounds of basketballs bouncing against the pavements; of people trying their best to make the most of the weather despite everything else going against them. Eager not to let Nycto destroy their lives. What was left of their lives, anyway.

"You hungry, Kyle?"

My mom's voice always made my stomach sink. Even when I was hungry, the thought of sitting at the table and eating with the people I'd nearly killed—all because of my stupid frigging naivety that'd blown my identity to Nycto in the first place—made any hunger slip away. "Nah," I said. "I'm good."

Mom didn't respond. But I heard the floorboards outside my bedroom door creak. I knew she was still standing there, trying to figure out what to say, to work out the right combination of words to pull me outta my stupor.

Truth was, there was nothing to say.

This was who I was. This was just the way it was.

"Well, we'll leave some leftovers for you. It's tikka. Your favorite."

The thought of tikka right now made me want to hurl. "Thanks, Mom," I said.

Again, a few more creaks of the floorboards.

And then Mom walked away, down the stairs, into the kitchen, the smells of tikka cutting through the smell of sweat in this bedroom.

I covered my face with my hands. Brushed back my greasy hair. I knew what my parents would think. I'd been through a lot. A hell of a lot. Gunman attack, ULTRA attack at the party venue. And all the baggage that followed. I was stressed. Course I was stressed. Everyone was stressed.

But they didn't know the half of it. They didn't understand my guilt. My shame. They never could.

Nycto's attacks were getting more and more sporadic, more and more random. But crucially, they were getting more and more deadly. Every time my heavy eyes refocused on the news, I'd see fresh footage of a flattened town, or skyscrapers tumbling down. I'd see tears in people's eyes. I'd see anger in the voices of protestors on the streets.

The worst thing of all?

Not only were they blaming Nycto for all this. They were blaming "Orion II," too.

"Orion II" was what they were calling me, by the way. Figured it worked. I'd tried to make myself look as much like Orion as possible. To them, I was nothing more than a name. A name of another dangerous entity. And even though I hadn't used my powers since the day I'd cast my outfit into the flames of Krakatoa, people claimed they'd seen me by Nycto's side when he attacked their cities, when he unleashed his rounds of destruction.

There were talks of Nycto being the most powerful ULTRA in existence. That he was some kind of experiment-gone-wrong; a leftover from the Era of the ULTRAs. The government spoke about the urge for human unity against the forces of Nycto and Orion II. That if we didn't stick together, as humans, and fight, then the world would fall. They were pretty clear about that.

Worst part? I couldn't disagree with them. They were right.

But I wasn't the one destroying the world. I was just a human, like everyone else. A human with a few party tricks. Party tricks that I was hopeless at using.

I saw the grainy footage of Nycto on the television and wondered why Daniel hadn't just exposed me. I could expose him, I knew that, but it'd only get me into trouble, raise questions and suspicions. But why hadn't he exposed me?

Then, it clicked. Of course he hadn't exposed me. He was enjoying his new power. Power came in many forms. Holding the secret identity of your arch rival? There were a lot of things you could do as an ULTRA, but there wasn't anything quite as terrifying as knowing that kind of info, especially when you had so much to lose.

Clearly Daniel didn't feel he had much to lose. If he had, he wouldn't have shown me his face in the first place.

He had all the leverage.

I heard the door slam downstairs. Heard footsteps coming up the stairs. I tucked my sweet popcorn under my bed quilt. Weird. Who'd be here for me at this time?

I felt the fear tingling within and did all I could to keep my powers under grips. Nycto. Was he here for me? Was the government on to me? Was someone else coming for me?

When my bedroom door flew open, it wasn't quite who I was expecting.

"Damon?"

Damon didn't look happy. In fact, he looked pissed. Pissed like I'd never seen him before. He didn't look me in the eye. He just looked around my bedroom. Looked at the mess on the floor. The empty crisp packets. The unwashed laundry. "Man, I'm just gonna say it. Just gonna say it as it is. But I miss you. We all miss you. Where the hell've you been?"

My mouth went dry. I hadn't seen Damon in almost three weeks. I'd been ignoring his calls. Ignoring his texts. Ignoring everything, everyone. I wasn't in the mood for people anymore. I wasn't in the mood for interactions.

Because everyone I was close to was at risk because of what Nycto knew.

"I've—I've just not been well."

"Man, none of us have been well. Not with all this Nycto crap goin' on."

The mention of Nycto made my head hurt. I didn't want to talk about him anymore. Spent enough time thinking about him as it was.

"We're your friends. And friends are supposed to look out for each other."

"Well, I appreciate you being here," I said. "Appreciate you checking in."

"No," Damon said, raising his voice even more. He was looking me right in the eyes now. "You just don't get it, do you? We... we miss you. Hell, we need you. You're our best friend, and that's what we all need more than anythin' right now. Friends. It's what... I need."

I wasn't sure it was possible to feel any guiltier than I did already. But hearing Damon's voice crack on those final words just about did it. "I'm sorry," I said.

"Well, good. You should be. 'Cause... 'cause you're being selfish."

"I've been ill—"

"Nycto's tearing the world apart, man. Him and that Orion II, they're tearing the world apart. And it's only a matter of time before they destroy New York, too. We're all in trouble. Every single one of us is in trouble. So now's not the time to be sitting around in our rooms staring at bullshit television. Now ain't the time to be sulking about what's happened, about what might happen. 'Cause... Kyle, I don't think we're gonna make it, man. I don't think any of us is gonna make it this time. There's no one out there. No one who can save us. No one strong enough. So we should be making the most of the time we've got. However... however long left that is."

Silence followed Damon's speech. I couldn't say anything if I wanted to.

"Call me," Damon said, walking away from my bed. "Please. Avi misses you. We all miss you."

He walked to my bedroom door. Stepped out of it.

"You look like total shit, by the way."

"Thanks," I said.

Damon let out a little laugh that reminded me of the way we always used to tease one another.

And then he stepped out of my room and disappeared down the stairs.

I looked at my open bedroom door. Inside, I felt my stomach turning. My muscles tightening. The fuzzy noise of Nycto's destruction on the television echoed around my mind.

But above anything, it was Damon's words that stuck with me.

There's no one out there. No one who can save us. No one strong enough. So we should be making the most of the time we've got.

I thought about my powers. I thought about what I was capable of. The powers I'd been cursed with.

And I realized right then that the Man in the Bowler Hat was right. He was right when he told me that I was weak, mentally. That it was dragging me down. Because I'd done amazing things when I'd been pushed. I'd fought off gunmen. I'd teleported around the world. I'd hurtled to the bottom of a volcano, frozen a pit of lava with my bare hands, got my parents home without as much as a scratch.

I'd done it because I cared about them. Because I loved them.

I'd done it because I'd had to do it. Because it was my duty to protect them. To save them.

Because I *could*.

I threw the quilt off my bed. Stepped onto my bedroom floor. The room around me grew clearer. The sunlight outside seemed warmer, stronger.

I stepped over to the window. Looked outside. Pulled open the window and breathed in the summer air. Listened to all the people out there chattering. The people playing basketball. The people doing what Damon said—making the most of what they thought were their final moments on earth. Because there was no one strong enough to take down Nycto. To protect them.

Except these weren't their final moments.

There was someone strong enough to protect them.

And he wasn't going to give up. Not anymore.

The time for hiding was over.

The time for fighting had begun.

36

I stood at the top of the Skytree in Tokyo and took a deep breath in.

The sky was dark. All around me, I saw lights. Cars driving through streets. The flashing neons of nightclubs. The smells of street food drifted right up to my position as the wind blew into me. I used to fear heights. Used to feel uncomfortable at heights.

Not anymore.

Not while I had a job. Not while I had a duty.

I focused on staying camouflaged in the darkness. Even if I weren't, it wouldn't matter. I was dressed in jet black. Even jetter black than I'd been in my old outfit.

But this wasn't just a replacement outfit. This wasn't a copy of Orion's outfit. I was done with being Orion II, with molding myself in someone else's image. I'd seen Nycto, and I knew the dangers that could bring.

No, now was the time to become a Hero. A new Hero.

I looked as far as I could see. Such a perfect city going about its everyday business. One of the cities I'd always wanted to see but was too afraid to step out of my comfort zone and actually explore.

But now, here I was. Here I was staring down at this city, as it braced for destruction. Because it would be destroyed, one day. If Nycto had his way, everywhere would be destroyed.

It was my duty to make sure that didn't happen.

I heard Damon's words in my head. *"There's no one out there. No one who can save us. No one strong enough. So we should be making the most of the time we've got."*

And I heard the Man in the Bowler Hat's words, too. *"If you can believe yourself, truly believe in yourself, you can achieve the one thing you've been gifted these abilities for."*

They resonated. They resonated now more than ever.

I wasn't weak. I had been weak, sure. When I was Kyle. When I was Kyle pretending to be Orion.

But now I was someone new.

Now, I was someone else entirely.

I looked down at my outfit. Black, again. Tighter fit. And on the chest of the long sleeved black latex shirt, a new emblem. A new symbol. One people would remember me by.

An eagle soaring, the light of the sun behind it.

I wasn't Kyle anymore. I wasn't Orion II.

I was Glacies.

And I was taking Nycto down.

37

Tommy Potts looked out of his bedroom window at the sunny street and wished he could play outside like the other kids.

It was hot. So hot. Usually, when it was hot, Mom let him go down to Central Park for a swim on weekends. She used to do it every single weekend it was sunny. He didn't have loadsa friends at school, so most of his best friends he'd made were down at that swimming pool.

He wished he could go make some more friends. But he wasn't allowed out today.

He craned his neck against the glass and looked down the road. The streets were usually busy, full of people. But they'd been quieter lately. Something to do with the ULTRAs. Tommy was only ten so he couldn't properly remember the ULTRAs, other than there was a big bang and that ended them. They seemed kinda cool, though. Even though they were nasty, there musta been some good ones. They were called Heroes at first, and Tommy was sure heroes were good things, so there must've been good ULTRAs, right?

He caught a whiff of the hotdog stands as he moved his nose

to the window, and he wanted to be out there so bad. It was his favorite kinda day. Sun shining, go out with Mom and get a hotdog then go paddling in the pool. Maybe even get a popsicle on his way home. He'd waited for days like these for so long. Now it didn't seem fair that he wasn't allowed, not after all this time.

Bill and Katie went to the pool on their own. They lived pretty close, so their parents said they trusted them, but Mom said their parents were "irresponsible" or something, even though Tommy didn't really know what that meant. All he knew was that he knew the way to the pool. He could get there, take a quick dip with some friends, then be back here without Mom ever even knowing. They liked to stay in bed late on a Saturday. He could be back here before they even woke up.

Tommy got so excited at the thought that he grabbed his swimming kit, already packed in his Nike bag. He pulled it over his shoulder, the butterflies all flapping around his body. He was doing this. He was gonna prove to Mom that he was a big boy and could do things like this for himself. They'd not like it while he was gone, but if he came back and told them he'd gone... they'd be so proud. They had to be so proud. And they'd let him go out on his own more often.

Tommy walked out of his bedroom. Slipped his trainers on by the door.

He stepped out into the hallway. Mom and Dad's door was never fully shut. He could see Mom in there. She was still. Totally still under the white sheets. Dad was at work at the One World Trade Center. He always worked early on weekends.

Tommy knew he had to go now. He couldn't waste any time.

He crept across the landing towards the top of the stairs. Every step felt heavier like it was closer to Mom finding out he was sneaking out. Even if she did, Tommy could just say he was going to the bathroom or something.

No. He couldn't wake Mom up. Special Agent Tommy. This was his mission.

He reached the top of the stairs and heard a floorboard creak in his parents' room.

Tommy froze. Stood there, bag over his shoulder. If Mom came out, they'd find him like this, and there'd be no way to explain himself. She'd know exactly what he was doing.

Tommy held his breath. Waited for a few seconds. Waited for Mom to walk out the room, head to the bathroom.

But she didn't.

The floorboard didn't creak again.

Tommy let go of his breath, those butterflies flying faster now. He climbed down the first step. Then the second. And before he knew it, he was at the bottom of the stairs, right by the front door.

He knew he needed a key. Mom and Dad said he wasn't old enough for a key yet. He'd have to borrow one of theirs. He'd be back before they knew he was gone.

He searched Mom's overcoat pocket and pulled out a key. He looked up the stairs again. Thought about climbing back up there, asking Mom if she'd take him. But he knew what she'd say. Same thing she'd said the last few days. It was too dangerous. Too dangerous with the ULTRAs around.

Yeah, well New York was fine still. Nobody had been hurt.

And a half hour wasn't gonna change much.

Tommy unlocked the door as quietly as he could. And then he turned the handle.

It snapped back up.

He stood rigid. His little heart raced. Stupid. Butterfingers. He had to be quiet. Had to make sure he didn't wake Mom.

Tommy turned the handle again, as hard as he could.

This time, it opened. He was outside.

Tommy stepped down the little path in front of his house, out onto the road. New York felt so much bigger when he was on his own. Like there were sounds in every direction, like the buildings were looking down on him, watching him.

But Tommy couldn't stand and stare. He had to get moving.

He walked down the sidewalk. Walked past a few people, all bigger than him. He thought he might stand out 'cause he was a kid, but people didn't even look at him. Maybe it's 'cause he was a secret agent. Maybe he was camouflaged! Special Agent Tommy at your service. It reminded him of the Mission Impossible films he watched with Dad. Tommy wanted to be like Ethan Hunt. This was his first mission.

He'd got to the end of the street when he saw some dark clouds ahead. Weird. The rest of the sky was completely blue and nice, just how he liked it. He started to worry that if it rained, they'd close up the pool, or everyone would leave and it'd be all for nothing 'cause he couldn't make any new friends.

But then he saw the crackle of lightning in the middle of the cloud.

He saw the figure floating there.

The figure dressed all in silver.

In its hands, flames.

Tommy dropped his swimming kit to the road and stared up as screams started to fill New York.

Nycto was here.

And he was getting ready to attack.

38

I t wasn't long before I heard the news that changed my life. I was in Great Piece Meadows, New Jersey. It was *called* a "meadow," but really it was more of a swampland. But it was quiet, so that's what I needed.

I was trying to figure out a pattern of Nycto's attacks, just like I had last time. But it was so warm, so sunny, that I could barely concentrate. Besides, it didn't seem like there were any patterns.

I didn't have to hear the news to know Nycto was in New York City. I saw it for myself. The dark cloud hovering in the distance, unlike anything I'd ever seen. I wasn't sure at first. Not right away.

Not until I saw the balls of orange burning in the sky, then crashing down into the city.

I felt a surge of adrenaline fill my body. Fear, sure. Felt like I wanted to heave, absolutely. But really, the feeling I felt more than any other was relief. Relief that I was finally being able to stand up to Nycto. That I knew exactly where he was.

Because now was the moment I stopped his madness. Now was the moment I stepped up to the plate.

Or at least, attempted to.

I bolted off the ground, outside the empty warehouse I'd been shacked up in. I became so conscious of myself as I flew through the sky. I knew people would see me. I knew they'd be just as fearful of me as they were of Nycto. And that wasn't their fault. It was just what they'd been trained. Not to mention the destruction they'd seen.

But that was something I just had to deal with right now.

I shot over onto Manhattan Island. The place was already well under attack. I saw glass flying out of the side of the Rockefeller. I saw people fleeing through Central Park as huge balls of orange flames blasted down on them. I saw entire streets crumble, cars falling through them.

These people. They needed help. They needed someone.

At the top of the island, I saw gunfire spraying upwards. The military. Quite a large military presence. They were firing everything they had at Nycto; shooting missiles into the sky. But Nycto wasn't even being scratched. The bullets just bounced off him. He threw the missiles back down to the ground.

I looked at Nycto, hovering there, feeling so invincible, and I felt anger. I felt pure rage. I wanted to stop him. To put an end to him right now while he wasn't expecting it.

But then I heard a scream down below.

When I looked at the road beneath me, I saw a boy. Young, probably only eight or so. He was holding someone. A woman, presumably his mother. He was trying to get her to move, crying as he attempted to wake her up.

Up above, I saw Nycto's hands filling with flames again.

If I didn't rescue that kid, he'd die.

I resisted the urge to fly at Nycto and I shot right down to the ground. In the corner of my eye, I saw Nycto's fireballs hurtling towards land. I kept my focus on that kid, on his unconscious—or worse—mother. I could do this. I could help him. Nobody else had to die today.

I saw the fireballs outpacing me and knew it was going to be tight. I didn't have long. And even if I did save this kid and his mom, there'd be so many others like him that I hadn't been able to save.

No.

I *could* save them. I could save everyone.

And that started with this boy.

I held my hands out in front of me as the fireballs shot past me. They were just meters from the little boy now. I saw them reflecting in his eyes. Saw the look of horror as they flew at him. Into him...

And then they stopped.

They froze.

I threw the fireballs—now snowballs—to the side. I landed by the boy and crouched beside him. He looked at me with fear, and I figured that must be something to do with my outfit—new, unfamiliar, but undeniably ULTRA.

"Come on, kid," I said, holding out my hand. "It's not safe for you here."

The kid blinked. Tears streamed down his cheeks. "My mommy," he said, holding onto her. "Please. I just wanted to go to the park and she... she came looking for me. But please. Please don't make my mommy go away."

I felt a lump in my throat and reached for the woman's neck. Around me, I heard more explosions, and that reassured me 'cause it meant Nycto had moved on. He thought he'd finished this kid off. That was a good thing. I wanted the element of surprise on my side when I finally took him out.

I felt a soft pulse in the woman's neck. "Your mom's gonna be okay," I said. "Take my hand. I'll take you someplace safe for now."

The boy sniveled. He hesitated a little, then took my hand.

I grabbed on to his mother and then I shot myself outside of New York City, into that warehouse I'd been in, in New Jersey, before the start of the attack.

"You wait here," I told the kid. "Don't go anywhere. Not until—"

"My dad," the boy said. "He... He was out there. In the World Trade Center. Please help him. Please."

I wasn't sure how to feel about the boy's demands. Part of me wanted to get on with fighting Nycto, finish him off. But another part of me felt a twinge of guilt, a flicker of familiarity. This boy was just like I was when I was younger. Looking for his dad, just like I'd been looking for my sister. His mom was in a bad way. I had no idea whether she was going to make it.

The best thing I could do for him was make sure his dad was okay. How hard would that be?

"Your dad," I said. "What's his name? What's he look like?"

"Peter," the boy said. "He's... He's got black hair. Tall. Thin."

"Narrows it down."

"What?"

I shook my head. "Nothing. Do you know what floor he works on?"

The boy squeezed his eyes shut, shook his head. "I... I went there once. I think it was fourteen. But I dunno. Just... please. Please help."

I sighed. "I'll do what I can for you, kid. What's your name, by the way? So I can tell your dad you're safe."

The kid sniveled. "Tommy," he said. "Tommy Potts."

"Tommy." I smiled at him. "I'll get your dad back to you. Promise. Now you just wait here."

I held my breath then I shot myself back into the Financial District, right outside the One World Trade Center. I could feel my teleportation powers getting stronger the more urgent this situation got. I could feel myself getting tougher like my powers were a muscle that I was training.

I hovered up to the fourteenth floor, where Tommy said his dad worked. I looked through the glass. Squinted for a sign of life. But there was no one there. I couldn't see a soul.

I started to hover around the side of the building to see if he was anywhere else on this floor when I became aware of a presence behind me.

I turned around.

Nycto was hovering opposite me, just meters away.

He was holding on to a man. A tall man with dark hair. Thin.

"Looking for someone?" Nycto asked.

He let go of Peter and dropped him to the ground below.

39

I watched Nycto drop Peter to the ground below and I felt the pain little Tommy would feel if I allowed this to happen.

I shot to Nycto's right to try and maneuver past him, but he shot in that direction even faster. I shot to his left, but still no luck. I was cornered. Cornered by my nemesis. He wasn't going to let me pass. Peter was going to hit the road.

"You've got nerve, Kyle," Nycto said. Hearing him say my real name reminded me of the real self underneath my costume, my disguise. "Thought you'd have learned your lesson back at Krakatoa."

Peter continued to hurtle to the ground below. I had no idea how Nycto knew I'd been trying to save Peter, reunite him with his child. I didn't have time to consider it.

"Me too," I said.

I shot downwards. Stretched my hands out. I fired the ice out in front of me, watched as it curled around Peter, softening his fall.

While I was holding on to Peter, I concentrated. Focused on

that warehouse back in New Jersey, where Tommy was waiting for him.

I felt my body shifting through space when something smacked into my back.

I fell down onto the road. Smacked my face right up against it. I felt the bones in my cheek crack, a sudden pain that only lasted a few seconds, and then I felt the bones rebuilding themselves as I rolled onto my back, turned around.

Nycto hovered over me. His hands were filled with flames.

"You should've learned your lesson," Nycto said. "You can't save humanity. We've tried reforming them before and it just never works. They never learn."

I watched the fireballs in Nycto's hands get larger. Peter was a few meters away from me. I needed to get to him. Quick.

"You're wrong," I said. I crawled towards Peter, the ice from my hands melting around him.

I heard Nycto chuckle. "Wrong about what?"

I stretched out. Grabbed Peter's arm. "I can save humanity. And I'll make them learn."

I saw Nycto's fireballs widen.

Leave his hands.

Hurtle down towards me.

I focused all my energy, all my attention, on getting back to that New Jersey warehouse, on getting Peter back to his son.

I squeezed my eyes shut and...

"Dad?"

I opened my eyes. I wasn't on that New York street anymore. My face felt better, not as painful. I smelled the musty air that I'd smelled not long ago.

"Tommy?"

I looked up and saw Peter run towards his son. Lift him up. I saw them smiling. Saw them crying.

But best of all, I saw Tommy's mom upright. Awake. Alive.

"Thank you," Peter said, turning around and looking right into my eyes. "Seriously. Whoever you are. Thank you."

I felt pride inside me. Felt a lump in my throat. As I stood there, I became more aware of myself, and I felt strong. Stronger than I'd ever felt in my entire life.

I'd done something. Something that'd earned the respect of someone. I'd done something that'd make my family proud. That made myself proud.

"I'll never let you down. Any of you."

I saw Peter open his mouth, prepare to say something else.

But before he could, I shot myself back to New York City.

I had work to do.

I LOOKED ALL AROUND for Nycto, but everything had gone quiet.

The streets were warm with the flames. I could smell smoke in the air. The sound of sirens surrounded me. Whenever I saw people, I camouflaged myself. They looked too scared to be thinking rational right now. Too fearful. If any of them saw me, they'd probably think *I* was Nycto.

But I'd saved people. I'd saved lives. I knew positive word would spread.

The streets of New York City seemed too quiet. I couldn't believe Nycto had just disappeared. He never gave up. He relished the fight. And, crucially, he felt he was stronger than me.

So where had he gone to?

What was he up to?

I thought about my family. My friends. And I felt sickliness in my stomach. I had to save people on these streets as Glacies. But I—Kyle, underneath—needed to know my family were okay.

They should be. Nycto's attack seemed limited to the main island, and my family and friends lived on Staten Island.

But Staten Island was close. Too close for comfort.

I looked over at Staten Island, over past the Statue of Liberty. Maybe I could just check in on them, quickly. Maybe I could just fly over there, check they were okay, then disappear. They'd probably be wondering where I was. Maybe it'd be better to show my face. Better to—

"Remember what I told you, Kyle?"

The voice came from behind me.

I turned around and saw Nycto standing in the middle of the road by the Staten Island ferry terminal.

"I warned you," Nycto said. "I warned you about what I knew. About what I'd do if you stood against me. Don't you listen?"

I fought through the urge to back down, to cower, that'd been with me all my life. And I said what I truly thought. "Why would I back down? I think it's you who should be backing down."

Nycto laughed. As he laughed, I felt electricity. A breeze. I saw litter lift from the ground, then hit it again when he stopped. "You really think you're strong enough? You really think you can defeat me in any way? They hate you. The people, the government, they hate you. You're fighting a losing battle. We're both the same to them. We're both freaks. So why don't you give up while you still have the chance? Why don't you listen to what I'm saying?"

I held my breath, and I walked up to Nycto. Shoulders slumped. Defeat filling my body, I stepped right up to him. Looked him in the eye.

"You know, for a super villain hell-bent on destroying the world, you really don't know when to shut your mouth, do you?"

Nycto hesitated. He didn't speak for a moment. "What—"

He didn't finish asking his question.

I punched him so hard, so full of anger, that the pair of us disappeared.

40

I punched Nycto as hard as I could and heard the second loudest explosion of my entire life.

I saw a blinding light all around me like I'd disappeared into the very middle of the sun. My ears rang. I could taste a hint of blood on my lips, smell a sweetness in the air. I had no idea where I was, how I'd ended up here.

I just knew that I'd punched Nycto and I'd teleported at the exact same time.

I'd punched him into another place.

And that was the very core of how I was going to defeat him.

The brightness disappeared from my eyes. I saw desert all around. Felt the blazing heat from above. I was in Arizona. Yes. That's it. I'd thought of Arizona right before I punched him. I'd thought of the desert, someplace well away from people, from Nycto's destructiveness.

And here I was.

I heard coughing, and it startled me from my thoughts.

Nycto was lying on the ground. Some of his silver armor had cracked and split. He looked up at me, coughing, smoke coming off his body.

"It's over," I said. "This madness, it ends. Right this second."

Nycto stared at me a few seconds, wincing. His leg looked bent out of shape. I wondered how good his healing powers were. How effective. Judging by the fact he was still lying there, I wagered a bet that they weren't as good as mine.

Maybe I was strong after all. Maybe I really was stronger than this monster.

"The murder. The destruction. All of it. It ends right here."

Nycto winced a few more times.

And then he started laughing.

"You shouldn't've done that," he said. "You really shouldn't've done that."

Quicker than I could think, Nycto sprung into the air. He flew into my chest. Knocked me back, off my feet.

I felt myself fly backward and heard a splitting explosion again. I saw the brightness, heard the ringing in my ears, and then I looked around and saw the familiar buildings and skyscrapers of New York. I was back here. He'd teleported me back here. He wasn't giving up. He wasn't down. Not yet.

"One thing you'll learn about me," Nycto said, pulling back his fist, "is that I never give up on something I've started. Never."

He went to plummet his fist into my face.

"Me neither," I winced.

I grabbed his fist and heard another explosion.

This time, when we came round, I was on top of him. We were in the jungle now. In the middle of the stifling hot rainforest, way away from any life, anything that Nycto could destroy.

I punched him in the face. Punched him as hard as I could, thinking of all the pain he'd caused people I cared about. Thinking about Mike Beacon. An enemy of mine at school, sure. But just another victim of Nycto's. Just another victim of Daniel Septer.

"You might think you're strong," I shouted. "But you're not. Not really."

I went to punch Nycto again and another deafening explosion threw us back into New York. This time, we were underneath the Statue of Liberty. Nycto smacked my head against it so hard that I heard the statue crack.

"I'm stronger than you are," Nycto said. "And unlike you, I don't have a thing to lose. How about we take a trip across the water, see if we can have a word with the people you care about?"

I thought of Mom, Dad, Damon, Avi, Ellicia, all my friends, as Nycto rammed my head into the feet of the Statue of Liberty once more. I held my breath. Focused all my attention on slithering out of his grip, teleporting right behind him and smacking him to the ground, then taking us far away again.

This time, we were in the sky. We were up in the clouds, high in the impossible winds. I saw commercial planes flying past right beside me. I felt the air thinning, impossible cold. But still I punched at Nycto. I kicked at Nycto. Because this was what I had to do. This was my duty. To defeat him. To rescue the people I cared about. To rescue everyone from mindless oblivion.

Eventually, after punching Nycto for a while, he flew back, out of my grip. I saw him faltering. Saw him falling through the sky like he was losing ground. I knew this was my chance. My chance to get him somewhere where I could finish him off once and for all. I had a place in mind. I just needed to time it right. I just needed to be quick.

I flew at Nycto. I flew at him and let the love and the anger and everything inside me power my final punch.

"You really should foolproof your own method before you use it," Nycto said.

I didn't know what he meant until I hit him.

Until he grabbed my hand and the explosion ripped through my mind once again.

When I opened my eyes, something was different.

I was underwater. Far underwater, the surface miles above me.

I could see Nycto drifting upwards. See him disappearing towards the surface. I couldn't breathe. I tried to use my powers to hold off the water, to hold my breath, but it wasn't easy. It wouldn't last forever.

I had to get out of this water.

I had to get away from Nycto.

I had to...

I tried to move my arms, but they were trapped. So too were my legs.

I looked around, and I saw why.

I was trapped. Trapped between rocks. Massive rocks at the bed of the sea, squeezing around my body, making it impossible to escape.

I watched Nycto rise to the surface. And as he rose, I swore I heard a voice in the back of my head. A tormenting voice in my mind, whispering out to me, taunting me, as I struggled between the rocks.

"You made a mistake, Kyle. And now the people you care about most will pay."

41

Ellicia stared at Facebook Messenger and felt her stomach turn.

Her curtains were drawn. Her room was pitch black. Most people had their televisions on, but she didn't. She could see images and videos of Nycto's attack on New York all over Facebook and Instagram as it was. She could hear it outside her window. The shouts. The screams. The destruction. She never really thought Nycto would get to her home city. Guess everyone who'd been attacked probably thought the same.

But now he was here, she wasn't sure she'd ever felt this afraid in her entire life.

And yet, despite everything, there was only one person she wanted to speak to right now.

The realization that she wanted to speak with Kyle, to make sure he was okay, hit her suddenly, soon after she'd seen the first building go down. She realized she was thinking about him. Hoping he was okay. And sure, he'd acted weird when she last saw him. He'd brushed her off like he didn't care. But the thing was, they'd all been through tough times. They'd all seen things, experienced things, that no sixteen-year-olds should have to. He was bound to be acting weird. Bound to be acting a bit, well, crazy.

But now, she just wanted to know he was okay.

She sent another message. Another one asking if he was okay. Again, no response. Which was weird. Whenever she sent messages in the past, Kyle would read them right away. He wouldn't reply to them right away—he'd start, she'd see the little ellipses at the bottom of the screen telling her he was working on something, he was trying to figure out what to say. But even though he took his time, he always read. He always replied.

Kyle's Messenger said he was last active forty-five minutes ago.

Nycto launched his attack forty-five minutes ago.

She felt a bit sick as she thought through the possibilities. Maybe Kyle was in New York City with his parents or his friends. Maybe he'd been there when Nycto and this other mystery ULTRA attacked. Maybe they'd stood in the view of the fireballs as Nycto launched his first attack...

No. She couldn't think that way. She didn't know that was the truth, not for definite.

It didn't seem good for Kyle. It seemed strange. But she didn't know anything for sure.

She scrolled back up her Instagram feed. More footage from the attack on New York. It looked like Nycto had given up his attack after taking down the Rockefeller, after searing Central Park, and he was now engaged in some kind of fight with another ULTRA. Nobody knew who this ULTRA was. Nobody knew what they wanted. The government spoke of the danger of all ULTRAs, the caution and vigilance to show towards all of them.

But Ellicia had read the stories. The stories of how this second ULTRA had saved people. Rescued people from burning buildings. Reunited children with their parents.

As much as the government wanted the people to believe all ULTRAs were bad, right now, it seemed like this guy in black was their only real hope.

Their final hope.

Ellicia put her phone down. She knew scrolling through Instagram was going to do no good. She had to get out. Find out if Kyle was okay. Sure, everyone was supposed to stay in their homes, but Staten Island hadn't been attacked. Besides, there'd been no concrete reports of attacks in a while now. A few false flags but nothing set in stone.

She walked over to her window. Peeked through the curtain. Kyle's place was about ten minutes away, but if she ran, she could get there in less than that.

She just needed to know he was okay. She just needed to check on him.

And that's exactly what she was going to do.

She turned around to walk out of her bedroom when she saw a shadow move behind the door.

She froze. There was nobody home. Mom and Dad were in Vermont with family for the weekend. They'd hesitated about leaving Ellicia here, especially with all the Nycto talk, but Ellicia had convinced them she'd be fine.

But there was someone in the house.

She crept slowly to the door. The silence inside the house suddenly seemed loud, like the quietness was crying out to her.

"Hello?" she called.

Nothing in response.

She cleared her throat. Maybe she'd just imagined things. She'd been through a lot of shocks lately, first with the attack at the soccer game, then at the party, now this. Seeing a few things was forgivable, understandable.

She walked out of her bedroom. Headed toward the stairs. Made a break for the door.

"Hello, Ellicia."

Ellicia's skin went cold. She recognized the voice, but she wasn't sure where from exactly.

She turned around and saw Daniel Septer standing in her hallway.

He was smiling. Smiling with a confidence she'd never seen on this weedy, scrawny kid from the year below.

"Dan... Daniel?" she said. There was something not right about this. Something off. "What're... What're you doing here?"

Daniel smiled at her. He looked too calm about this. Too at ease.

It was then that she noticed what Daniel was wearing. What covered him from toe to neck.

That dark silver armor.

The armor just like... Nycto.

Ellicia froze. She froze right there as she realized. She didn't want to believe it. Didn't want to accept it.

But she could only believe what she saw in front of her.

Daniel Septer was in her house.

Daniel Septer was Nycto.

"Well?" he said. "Aren't you gonna run?"

Ellicia stayed still for a moment.

Held her breath.

Then she swung around. Grabbed the handle of the front door. Started to lower it.

Something grabbed her hand. Snapped it away from the handle. And before she could scream, a warm hand covered her mouth.

"I wouldn't if I were you," Daniel said.

In his other hand, burning bright, a fireball.

"Time to see how much your dearly beloved really cares about you."

He moved the fireball closer to Ellicia's face.

42

I'd never liked being submerged underwater. Never.

But being submerged at the bottom of the ocean, surrounded by rocks, pinning you into place?

Yeah. That was a whole lot scarier than a bit of water to the face.

I could see the light on the surface of the water. I was freezing. Icy cold. I'd already been holding my breath for what must've been minutes. And as strong as I was, as strong and powerful as I knew I was, I wasn't sure how much longer I was going to be able to hold on.

My ears were so clogged up. Something people don't tell you about the ocean. It isn't completely silent like you'd expect it to be. There is a sound to it. A gentle hum like the water itself is singing.

It might've been calm if I wasn't struggling for my life.

I focused my attention on my love for my family, my friends. I focused my anger on Nycto. But no matter how much I tried to shift the rocks around me, I just couldn't do it. And changing that focus made it trickier for me to hold my breath. I could feel myself gasping, and I knew what was happening. I was beginning to drown. I was going to drown down here, and Nycto was going to destroy everything, everyone I cared about. Then the rest of the world.

I was the only one who could stop him, and I was trapped underwater.

I tried moving again. But it seemed like the water was dulling my powers. I felt like Kyle. Not like Glacies. I didn't feel powerful. I felt weak. I felt fear building up inside me. Fear and panic. What had I done? Why couldn't I have just stayed in my room like everyone else? My powers weren't a gift. They were a curse. I didn't have a duty to anyone but myself. I was just a kid. I had a life ahead of me. Sure, it might've been a shitty life ahead if Nycto had his way, but it was a life nonetheless.

Well, not now. Not anymore.

I kept on struggling against the rocks, fighting to free myself, but I was fast becoming aware of just how desperate, how hopeless, my situation was. And that terrified me. It terrified me as I let bubbles of air out, my already enhanced lungs pushed to their limits. It terrified me as I tried to teleport away from here, but could only manage to shift myself for a split second before gargling more water.

I stared up at the surface. Stared at the sun as it rippled on it. It was quite peaceful, really. Hearing the song of the water. Listening to the hum of stillness. And as I opened my mouth and let out more air bubbles, the last few air bubbles I had, I started to think that maybe this wasn't so bad after all. Maybe it wasn't the worst way to go. After all, even if I did survive, I wouldn't be able to stop Nycto. Nycto was too strong. Nycto was...

I heard the Man in the Bowler Hat's voice in my mind.

"If you can believe yourself, truly believe in yourself, you can achieve the one thing you've been gifted these abilities for."

And then I heard the desperation Damon had spoken with.

The need to just spend time with me, as a friend. The acceptance that the world was ending, and he just wanted to make the most of the last days.

But it didn't have to be that way.

It really didn't have to be that way.

I let out the final air bubbles from my lungs. There wasn't any air left inside me anymore. I could feel my brain crying out for me to open my mouth, to swallow the water, to inhale it all in. But I told myself I couldn't do that. I couldn't let the water in. My brain was tricking me. Breathe in and I died. Hold on for as long as possible...

I saw the sunlight above getting brighter and it felt warm. My muscles weakened. I wanted to hold on, but I wanted to relax more. Relax here at the bottom of the sea, with the stillness, with the humming music.

I wanted to drift away with the water.

I felt like I'd been here before. Like I'd been submerged underwater when I was very young, a long time ago.

Voices muffled.

Someone standing over me.

I wanted to close my eyes.

I wanted to slip away.

I wanted to...

I saw my sister right in my mind. Clearer than I'd ever seen her before.

I saw the explosion Saint set off when Orion hit him. I saw the blast, and then I heard my parents' screams.

They became the screams of everyone else. The screams of children like Walt, who just wanted to know where his dad was. The screams of parents, desperate to keep their children safe.

The screams of innocent people.

Of my friends.

I couldn't give up on them. I couldn't just throw the towel in.

As my vision blurred, as the strength slipped out of my body completely, I found one final ounce of strength inside me to tense my fists, squeeze my eyes together, grit my teeth together, embrace every bit of love and hate I'd ever felt inside me, as strong and as powerful as I possibly could.

And then I...

43

E   llicia felt Nycto's grip tighten around her neck even
     though he didn't have his hands anywhere near her.
          She was in her living room. It was completely
pitch black, the curtains pulled over. It was never usually this
dark, so Nycto must've done something. He was called Nycto
after all, which apparently meant "night."

She could hear talking on the streets. Police cars blaring
sirens. Cries and whimpers. And she just wanted to scream. To
cry out, beg someone to come in here and help her.

But every time she tried, Nycto's invisible grip just got
stronger.

She was trapped. She was alone.

And she was going to die in here.

"You know, things could've been different," Nycto said. It
was strange hearing him speak with that deep voice of his. He
had his mask on again, taking the Daniel Septer away, turning
him back into that stronger version of himself. Because Daniel
Septer was always a weak kid who'd been bullied. Ellicia never
really had anything against him. He was just a year younger, so

she didn't have much to do with him. She kind of felt sorry for him, in truth. Wanted to see him stand up for himself.

But not like this. Not like this at all.

"I gave him a choice," Nycto said. "A choice between backing down, letting me get on with my work. Or... well. This."

Ellicia didn't know what Daniel was talking about. She wanted to be able to ask, but she couldn't even breathe. She could feel her legs starting to shake. Feel her lungs gasping for air. She knew it was almost over. She was ending here.

But what was this all about?

What was any of this about?

He'd mentioned Kyle earlier. But what did Kyle have to do with anything? Maybe he'd upset Daniel although Ellicia didn't think so. Kyle wasn't the kind of guy who upset anyone. He'd been through crap himself, not exactly gonna start making another guy's life a misery.

"Oh. You don't understand, do you? I mean, you really don't know the truth?"

Ellicia's vision started to fade. She wanted to hold on. To hold on so she could hear what Nycto had to say. To hear what the "truth" Daniel spoke about was.

"Our new friend. The one fighting me. You've seen him, right?"

Ellicia's mind drifted to the second ULTRA from today's mayhem. The one who'd been fighting Nycto, who'd saved so many people. She felt calm when she thought of him. She'd heard so many good things. Maybe he'd be able to help people in the long run. Maybe he'd be able to fight Nycto. To stop him causing more hell.

But her time was up.

Her life was over.

She was terrified. Sad. Angry.

But her time was up, and she had to stay strong, just like

Mom would've wanted her to. She wished she'd gone with her and Dad to Vermont. She'd have felt safer there.

She wished she'd been able to go with Kyle. To take him with her.

She hoped he was okay. Prayed that no matter what, he was okay.

"Of course you've seen him," Nycto said. "Gallivanting around New York and the rest of the world like it's his playground." He spat. "I gave him a choice. You have to understand that. I gave him a choice to either join me or back down. So don't blame me for this. Blame him. He caused this."

In her drifting mind, she pictured the good ULTRA swooping in, saving her life.

"He isn't coming for you, Ellicia," Nycto said like he was reading her thoughts. "He isn't coming for anyone. No-one is. I'm sorry you won't be around to enjoy the fireworks. But I'm going to create a beautiful world. A new world. A world where no one can stamp me down again. No-one."

Her vision blurred.

Her head spun.

"So say goodbye," Nycto said. "Say goodnight. It won't be long now. The darkness is coming. The darkness is—"

Then, something happened.

44

I didn't think anymore.

    I didn't dwell on the past. I didn't feel love. I didn't feel anger.

I didn't feel anything.

I just felt an urge. One overriding urge, dominating everything.

Defeat Nycto.

Finish him for what he'd done.

I dragged myself out of the water. Flew right to New York. And even though I didn't know where he was exactly, somehow, I did. It was like I had a honing device on Nycto, and I knew where he was, what he was doing. I could feel Ellicia's fear. I could feel her struggling. And he wasn't going to get away with this. I was going to make sure of that.

I worried I was too late as I flew faster than I thought was possible through the sky, damp and drenched, towards Ellicia's. I worried that I'd failed. That I'd let myself, everyone down, all over again.

But that worry was soon covered up when I crashed through the front of Ellicia's house.

Slammed into Nycto's side.

Sent him hurtling out of the back of Ellicia's house, miles and miles into the distance.

I wanted to know Ellicia was okay. I wanted to know she'd made it. But I didn't have time for that. Not right now.

The important thing was, I had Nycto. I'd caught him off guard.

I was crouching over him.

He looked up at me as he lay there, broken on the grass. The bottom half of his silver mask had ripped away, and I could see Daniel Septer' smile underneath. "You're... you're strong," he said. "Stronger than I thought. But still not as strong as me."

He powered a punch into my gut and the pair of us hurtled into the sky.

I punched back. Teleported around him, dodging every hit I could, and he did the same. We dodged planes. We dodged buildings. We even dodged missiles that the military fired up at us. It was like a dance. But this wasn't just any old dance. It was a dance to the death. A dance that only one of us was getting out of.

I slammed a fist into Nycto's face. I felt his bone crunch, and I saw him wobble out of the way. I pounded into his chest, feeling it break upon contact as the pair of us fell from the sky, back towards the ground.

"You're wrong," I shouted. "You aren't stronger than me. You never will be stronger than me."

I teleported us away from New York City, away to the only location I knew I could go.

But Nycto grabbed me and teleported us back. I could see Staten Island approaching as we alternated our teleportation. I could see my house. My home, right near us. And then right below us.

"That's where you're wrong," Nycto said.

He kicked me in the stomach and bounced down to Sherman Avenue, right in front of my house.

His hands turned orange, flames simmering out of them. He looked up at me, half of his mask ripped away. I could see something on his chest. Something burning. Flames, similar to the light that burned from Saint's chest when Orion powered into him.

"Can you feel it?" Nycto shouted, his voice echoing into the sky. "Can you feel the power I feel?"

I saw the ground shaking underneath Nycto. I saw litter, debris, all of it moving towards his hands, just like it moved towards Saint before The Great Blast. Inside the house, I saw Mom and Dad peeking through the curtains. Looking at Nycto. Then looking at me as I hovered over. I saw more terrified eyes in the houses and flats around me. More horrified faces at the truth of what was happening all over again.

There was going to be another Great Blast.

It was the only way I could defeat Nycto.

"You see, you could end it," Nycto said. "You could end everything right here. But you won't. Because you're too attached. Too attached to your family. Too attached to the people around you. You could end me, right here. But you're too weak."

"I'm stronger than you'll ever be."

"Then prove it," Nycto said. His voice grew louder. Lightning flashed in the sky above. The fireballs in his hands were twice the size of basketballs now, and getting bigger by the second. "Prove you have what it takes. Prove you're willing to give up everything to take me down. If that's what being an ULTRA really means to you, then prove it."

I looked through the window of my house again. I saw my parents. I knew they'd be terrified. And I knew that if I threw myself at Nycto, used all the power I had, I'd not only destroy

Nycto, myself, but I'd kill thousands of people, too. Maybe millions.

Was that the legacy I really wanted to leave behind?

Was that really what I wanted people to remember me by?

"You don't have it in you," Nycto said, laughing now. As he laughed, his voice cracked, and I heard Daniel underneath. Daniel, enjoying this, corrupted by power.

"You know, you were right about one thing," I said.

Nycto smiled. The fireballs were beaming electricity now. The sky had turned jet black as a whirlwind spun around the street, making the electricity flicker everywhere. "Go on."

"Back at Krakatoa. You told me we weren't so different. I didn't believe you at the time. I didn't want to believe you. But now I see what you mean. We aren't so different. Not underneath our masks."

Nycto smiled. "If you're trying to talk your way into allegiance, you've missed your opportunity."

I smiled back. "Don't worry. It's not allegiance I'm looking for. It never was."

I took in a deep breath and let every emotion fill my body, shake my core.

I felt cold ice build at my hands. I felt it cover my body. I felt it freezing around my chest.

"We're the same in that we've both been trodden down by the world. We were both losers, before all this. But you know what the difference between us is?"

Nycto smiled some more. I could barely hear him through the intense barrage of noises we were both creating. "Enlighten me."

I pointed my hands forward. "I'm Glacies," I shouted. "And I gave up crying like a little bitch at the way the world treated me. You never did."

I threw myself at Nycto.

Held my breath.

And at the last moment, the last instance before we collided, I looked my parents in the eye and felt pure raw love.

"I love you," I said, tears rolling down my cheeks.

And then, without touching Nycto, I felt the environment around me change to the only place I could think of.

"Hey, Daniel?" I said.

His fireballs weakened. He looked around, startled. "What—"

"Thanks for showing this place to me. Enjoy your time here."

I slammed into Daniel and sent him flying down into the mouth of Krakatoa.

I felt him try to fight. Try to shift his way out of my hands, away from my grip. I felt him try to teleport us out of here, back to New York. I felt him try to explode.

But I held on.

I held on with every ounce of power I had.

I held on as we flew down into the volcano.

As the heat intensified.

As the lava pit approached.

I held on as rocks fell around us.

As debris flew at my face.

I held on right until we hit the lava.

And then, only then, did I release every single ounce of power inside me.

The blast of ice ruptured the volcano.

Rocks flew everywhere, destroying the natural wonder, closing the entrance.

But I wasn't scared. I wasn't afraid. Not anymore.

Because I was Glacies. And Glacies couldn't be afraid.

I saw the light surround me.

Felt coldness cover my every inch.

And as the volcano collapsed around me, shattered by my blast of power, I felt truly proud. Truly at peace.

Truly Heroic.

"**M**an, you slept through *this* shit? How the hell does anyone sleep through *this* shit?"

I sat on Damon's sofa. Avi was beside me holding on to his new iPad Pro, how he'd afforded it I had no idea. I was completely stuffed after what must've been my fiftieth pizza of the week. Yeah, my appetite had grown since I'd taken down Nycto. Saving the world had a funny effect like that.

I watched the video of the events unfold. Some genius video editor had compiled all the known footage of the battle, edited it together like a movie. In truth, I felt a bit conscious when I saw myself on that screen. Like someone would notice it was me. Figure it out.

But... nah. To the world around me, I was still just Kyle Peters. Still just the weak-ass who fake-shat himself at school. Still just the idiot who slept through the greatest ULTRA showdown since the last Era of the ULTRAs.

"And that punch, man." Damon smacked a fist into his palm. "Ugh! That *slug!*"

I watched the final moments of the known footage. The

moment where I got all charged up, as too did Nycto. I saw myself fly at him, then the pair of us just disappear for the final time into thin air. The incident that occurred right before the freak eruption of Krakatoa. The most devastating eruption of all time.

Only, everyone had survived it.

Some genius blocked the lava flow, redirected it. A miracle, people of nearby islands said. An impossibility.

Some people said it was God's work. I felt a little arrogant taking credit for that, so I was just happy they'd made it out alive.

Nycto, however...

"Dude, gotta worry about that Glacies, though," Avi said.

"Why?" I asked. I was pretty smug that people were referring to Glacies by his name. I figured I'd shouted it before I rammed myself into Nycto. For the first time in my life, I had a cool nickname that didn't involve my lankiness, my general crappiness, or fake-shitting myself. "He seemed to do a pretty good job of sorting Nycto out. It's been three weeks since we last heard anything."

Avi nodded, chomping down on popcorn. "That's what I mean. He seemed a straight up guy. Someone who wanted to do good by us. Damn. He mighta been a hero."

He mighta been a hero indeed.

"Whaddya reckon actually happened?" Avi asked. "When those two disappeared. Where'd they go?"

I didn't like to think too much about those final moments. I hadn't enjoyed throwing Nycto into the lava pit, freezing it over. It was made even worse by the fact that his mask slipped away at the last moment, and I saw Daniel's fearful eyes staring up at me, just like he used to when he was trodden on and bullied back at school.

But I'd done what I had to do. I'd dealt with the greatest

threat to humanity since the Era of the ULTRAs. It wasn't nice. It wasn't pretty. But it was the right thing to do. The only thing to do.

"I mean, you reckon they're dead?" Avi asked.

I shrugged. Stuffed my hand in the popcorn box and crunched some. "Wherever they are, I like to think Glacies won. 'Cause we haven't heard from Nycto in ages. That's gotta mean something."

Avi dragged the popcorn back. The three of us sat there, watching the footage unfold. "Yeah, that's somethin' alright."

The weirdest, most unexpected development in all this was the way Glacies was being talked about. Social media were going mad with stories of the people who'd been saved. Even the president, in his speech, thanked Glacies for dealing with the Nycto threat, but urged him, if he was alive, to hand himself in for the good of all mankind. Of course, I wouldn't be doing that. Not at all.

But I was going to make sure I was ready in case I ever needed to use my powers again.

"So, there's a new milkshake place open," Avi said.

"Another?" Damon said. "Damn. Don't they ever give up on those places?"

"Hey,' Avi said, raising his hands. "Don't knock the milky shakes, man. Do not knock the milky shakes."

Damon and Avi play-fought for popcorn, and I just sat there smiling. I could go for milkshake. I could do normal things. The things a sixteen-year-old guy was supposed to do. I could finish school, go back to being teased again. Why? Because I'd stepped up when I needed to. Because I'd believed in myself, just like the Man in the Bowler Hat told me to.

"If you can believe yourself, truly believe in yourself, you can achieve the one thing you've been gifted these abilities for."

I saw right now that he was absolutely right.

Wherever he was, whoever he was, I owed it all to him.

We left Avi's place and walked down the sun-soaked street. The air smelled like street food again, like it did before the Nycto panic. People traveled over on the boat from Manhattan, tourists, all looking happy about their lives, all living in something like normality all over again. Because it was. Things were normal again. And sure, something big and bad would probably come along again one day. But right now? Things were good. And that was all that mattered.

"Kyle?"

I heard the voice from behind me.

When I turned around, all my confidence, all my fearlessness, drifted away.

Ellicia was standing there. She was on her own, a strawberry milkshake in hand.

I thought about just waving back and pretending I hadn't seen her. The nervy old Kyle inside told me that'd be the right thing to do, even though Damon was jabbing at me to go talk to her, and Avi was chatting about how she was a "fine broad", whatever that meant.

But I fought through my nervousness and walked toward her.

"Hey," I said, scratching the back of my neck.

"Hey," she said back. She looked at the sidewalk. "How you doing?"

"Yeah, I'm good. You?"

"Yeah," she said, looking back up at me. Her eyes glistened in the sunlight.

"Well, that's good. We're both good. Good thing we're both good."

She sniggered. I wasn't sure how idiot I sounded on a scale of one to idiot, but I wagered I was right up there in idiot territory.

"You guys off somewhere?"

"Oh," I said, looking back at my mates. Damon waved. Avi stood in his "cool" pose, hands on his hips, obviously eager to impress. "Yeah, we're just heading to check out that new milkshake place."

"Oh. Well. I've got milkshake. I like milkshake."

I nodded at her milkshake. "So I see."

We both smiled. Then both looked at the sidewalk. And by the looks of things, we both blushed.

"Anyway," I said. "I'd better..."

"Yeah," Ellicia said. "Enjoy."

"I'll try. Thanks."

I turned around and walked after my friends. But as I walked away, I felt that same sense of disappointment I'd always felt when I didn't say what I truly wanted to with Ellicia. When I didn't just say how I really felt, what I really wanted.

I was a dork. There was no way I was getting anywhere with her.

She didn't really like me. It was all in my head.

I might as well just...

I stopped. Took a deep breath of the fresh summer air.

I turned around. Fought past the voices, the monsters in my mind, and looked back at Ellicia as she walked away, milkshake in hand.

"Hey!"

Ellicia stopped. She turned around.

"Say you, erm. You like milkshakes?" God, man. Just say it. Just ask the damned girl!

"I can't stand them," Ellicia said, a deadpan smile on her face.

"Oh," I said. "Well... It's just—"

"I'm feeling sick after this one. But I'd love to spend some time with you, yeah."

She walked towards me. As she did, I felt tingling in my fingers, all over my body. If I didn't keep my cool, I'd end up hopping thirty feet in the air right now.

I tried to control my beaming smile as Ellicia joined me, and as we caught up Damon and Avi.

I felt her fingers brush against mine as we approached the milkshake place. And as we walked together, hand in hand, I felt like everything in my life was complete.

I felt like everything in my life was perfect.

"If you can believe yourself, truly believe in yourself, you can achieve the one thing you've been gifted these abilities for."

He'd been right. The Man in the Bowler Hat had been right. Whoever he was, he'd been right.

I looked up into the sky and muttered "Thank you," under my breath.

"What?" Ellicia asked.

I smiled at her. Squeezed her hand, feeling its warmth. "Nothing."

The pair of us walked together towards the milkshake place.

"If you can believe yourself, truly believe in yourself, you can achieve..."

Mostly true.

Although I'd still not figured out how the hell I was supposed to start a conversation with the girl of my damned dreams, yet.

[46]

He watched the boy walk into the milkshake place, the girl's hand around his.

He felt a little mad about that. After all, he'd warned him. He had to shed the idea of being Kyle Peters if he wanted to make it in this world. The boy couldn't lead a double life. He knew—he'd tried leading a double life, and it was no way to live. It wasn't fair. It only led to pain. Destruction.

But as he perched atop the building opposite, he saw the smile on Kyle's face, and he couldn't intervene. He just couldn't. The kid had been through a lot. And he'd done good. He'd not only survived, but he'd conquered. He'd proven he had the mental strength to defeat his physical strength. He'd proven he was more than just an ULTRA—he was a Hero.

But as he watched Kyle smile, he couldn't help but pity him. Walking around like this was all over. Well, it wasn't over. It was never over.

He'd find that out very soon.

"Watching him again?"

He turned around. Angel was standing there, hands on her

hips. Her bleached white hair hung down onto her shoulders. She never looked a day older every damned time Bowler saw her.

"You should be careful flapping your wings in public," he said.

"Ever the charmer, Bowler. What's up with this kid, anyway?"

Bowler looked down at the entrance to the milkshake place. Watched Kyle step inside. "He did well. Defeating Nycto."

"Hell, he did more than well. He risked everything using his powers. Way more than any of us managed."

"We have a reason to fear using our powers," Bowler said. "And Glacies will discover that too. In time."

"Let's just hope he doesn't find out the hard way."

A lump swelled in Bowler's throat. "Let's."

He stared over at the milkshake place and then looked beyond it. Looked at this city. This perfect city.

"There will come a time when we have to rise again," Bowler said. "For real."

"You feel the storm approaching, too?"

"Stronger than ever."

"And when it does?"

Bowler looked back down at the milkshake place. "We're going to need all the help we can get."

Memories flooded his mind. Memories of the past eight years. Of everything that had happened. The silent battles. Battles with the government. Battles with... others.

"Two new ones in the space of a few weeks," Angel said. "Extra-powerful ones, too."

Bowler waited a few seconds. She didn't continue. "And?"

"Don't you think it seems, well... weird?"

"Not particularly."

"But doesn't it make you wonder? Just a little?"

Bowler didn't want to answer Angel just yet. There'd be a time. There'd be a place. But right now... right now it wasn't so important.

"Want me to go have a chat with our new friend?" Angel asked. "I could show him what I can do. Sure to be a date-killer."

Bowler half-smiled. "Not now. Let the boy have his fun. He'll need it if he's to be ready for what's coming."

Angel whistled. "Wow. Bowler showing patience with a newbie. Never thought I'd see the day."

Bowler sighed. "Me neither."

"What is it with this kid then? Really? I sense... something different."

Bowler swallowed a lump in his throat. He had flashes back to the day. The day everything changed. The day he'd made the most difficult decision of his life.

"Nothing," Bowler said, adjusting his bowler hat. He felt stifling hot in all this gear. But there was nothing he could do about that. He had a disguise to keep. "Guess I'm just softening in my old age."

Angel slapped Bowler across his arm with her talons. "Chin up, sport. Now's not the time to be gettin' soppy. Anyway. Gotta shoot. Things to do. Life to live."

"Yeah. Later."

As Angel disappeared off the roof of the building, Bowler stood there a little longer, staring out at the New York skyline over the Hudson River, then back down to the streets, then to the milkshake place below.

He was glad he still had his mask on. Because he definitely didn't want Angel to see that he was crying. Not that she could see him anyway. Nobody could.

If she'd seen him, she'd have seen the truth.

But nobody could know the truth.

Nobody could know he was Orion.
Nobody could know that he'd survived the Great Blast.
And nobody could know the truth about Kyle Peters.
His biological son.

WANT MORE FROM MATT BLAKE?

The second book in The Last Hero series, Rise of the ULTRAs, is now available.

Word-of-mouth and reviews are crucial to any author's success. If you enjoyed this book, please leave a review. Even just a couple of lines sharing your thoughts on the story would be a fantastic help for other readers.

If you want to be notified when Matt Blake's next novel in The Last Hero series is released, please sign up for the mailing list by going to: http://mattblakeauthor.com/newsletter Your email address will never be shared and you can unsubscribe at any time.

mattblakeauthor.com
mattblake@mattblakeauthor.com

Made in the USA
Coppell, TX
11 October 2021

63860224R00150